Rhoda

Elizabeth Novey

Proverbs 3:5-6

Rhoda

Elizabeth Novey

Oak Hill Academy Publishing

Wyocena, Wisconsin

Cover design: Elizabeth Novey, Laura Novey

Cover illustration: Elizabeth Novey

Cover photography: Laura Novey

Back cover portrait: Used with permission. ©Lifetouch Inc.

All Scripture references are from
the King James translation.

Oak Hill Academy Publishing

Wyocena, Wisconsin

To the One
who has shone His Light
in my own heart
(2 Corinthians 4:6)

Contents

"[God the Father] hath delivered us
from the power of darkness,
and hath translated us
into the kingdom of his dear Son:
In whom we have redemption
through his blood,
even the forgiveness of sins."
~Colossians 1:13-14

Introduction:
The Letter

Rhoda rocked back and forth in the antique rocking chair, lips drawn tightly, listening to the soft scratching of the pen as Mother composed the letter. She hoped with all her might that the mailman wouldn't come, the letter be lost, the receiver decline. Rhoda sighed in despair. Soon, she and her siblings would be sent away from home to live with strangers. Of course, it would only be temporary, Mother had promised, but the very thought of it rested heavily on her thin shoulders, infecting her eleven-year-old mind with worry.

Making it all the weightier was the darkness—that thick blackness that blocked out the faces of her family, the beauty of the countryside, the magnificence of the pictures that Anna could draw so well. Anything out of place frightened her when its unfamiliar form touched her fingers or tripped up her feet. The blindness had struck unexpectedly several months before.

All through Rhoda's illness, Mother had been near her daughter's bedside. Mother had entertained her with captivating stories when Rhoda was tired of lying in bed all day. She had consoled her when the fever stole away her sight. It was not surprising, then, that when Mother received the news that her niece, Charity, had fallen gravely ill, she decided at once to help. Life had been a struggle for Aunt Bette ever since her husband had left to find work.

The main hindrance was the question of where the children should be taken. Mother would not permit them to go along with her due to the risk of contracting the illness. That was how the idea formed to write a letter to Pastor and Mrs. Olson to see if they might take the children for a while. Mother had not seen them for years, but she was fairly certain they would consent. Her suspicion was confirmed by a letter that came in the mail a few days later.

Rhoda's heart was torn in two. She knew that Mother had to go to help Aunt Bette, but she hated the idea of being separated from Mother so far from home. Regardless, her mother had made up her mind.

"Rhoda, dear, we mustn't think only of ourselves. Aunt Bette needs my help caring for Charity. Don't you think it's for the best?"

"But Mother, I need you. Who will take care of me?" Rhoda's chin began to quiver, but she clenched her teeth and tried to scowl.

Mother held her daughter close and tucked her hair behind her ears. "Mrs. Olson is a very kind woman. She and your sisters will take good care of you while I'm gone."

Rhoda couldn't argue. They would depart the following morning.

Chapter One:
The Olsons

"Mrs. Olson?" inquired Mother hesitantly, not quite remembering the appearance of her old friend. She stepped off the train, followed by Anna, Rhoda, Ruth and Elijah, all loaded down with luggage. The train hissed a farewell to the family as it chugged out of the station.

"No, of course not," the woman huffed in disdain. Smiling stiffly, she added, "I'm Lucille Maxwell. Pastor Olson is making a house call, so I told Rebecca that I'd meet you at the station."

"I see," Mother replied. "I'm sorry to cause you to go to so much trouble just to come and pick us—"

"Don't be sorry, Mrs. Clayton. Poor Rebecca feels terribly about not being able to meet you at the train station. Quite naturally, I told her that it wouldn't be out of my way at all to come and get you myself. It's my duty to my dear friend, and my pleasure, too. It wasn't any trouble at all." Without even stopping for a breath, the woman motored on. "You see, I was out and about anyway running errands at the general store and the post office. I stopped by to visit my husband, too. He owns the bank, you know. Where does your husband work? Oh, how insensitive of me. I remember Rebecca telling me that he passed away in recent years. I'm sorry to hear of your loss, Mrs. Clayton."

Mother didn't respond. Rhoda knew that Lucille Maxwell had struck a nerve.

"The car is parked right over here." Mrs. Maxwell's tall heels clicked on the pavement as she took short, brisk steps toward a gleaming Franklin V-12. "Put your bags in back. Walter and I just got a new, larger car. It's not a Packard limousine, mind you, but it serves its purpose."

3

The Clayton clan tramped to the car and neatly placed their carpetbags and Mother's clutch purse inside. Mrs. Maxwell looked the family up and down through her piercing gray eyes. She gave a forced smile that dripped with dissatisfaction at what she saw. They were all dressed in well-worn, yet clean, feedsack clothes. All but Rhoda were sunburned. Pulling a small mirror from her handbag, Mrs. Maxwell began to adjust her already-perfect hair and reapply her lipstick. She was decked out in a close-fitting yellow dress that flared in pleats around the bottom of the skirt. Positioned on her head was an asymmetrical, brimless felt hat with a single feather dipping to one side.

As the children clambered into the back seat, Ruth whispered to Rhoda, "She must be rich. Her car's the fanciest one I ever seen, an' she's wearin' a swanky dress. I wonder if she always gets all dolled-up, or if it's just when she meets people at train stations."

Anna snickered in a hushed tone at Ruth's last comment. She whispered an explanation. "Her husband's the banker. They ought to be rich. They can afford such things."

As the car pulled away from the station, the children continued their muffled conversation.

"Did you see the way Mrs. Maxwell looked at Mother?" Ruth leaned in closer to her siblings and continued. "Maybe it's 'cause Mother don't have a store-bought dress and ain't got her hair all done up."

"Doesn't have," corrected Anna.

"I'm glad we don't hafta live with her," Elijah muttered, wrinkling up his pudgy nose.

Rhoda focused her attention on the rich woman's continuous monologue.

"I have two little boys, Dick and Andrew. Dick is nearly six, and Andrew just turned five last month. They are the plague of my life at times, I tell you. Look at your children, so well behaved. Then there are my boys. I can hardly get a moment's peace! I just don't understand it. We give them all the best that money can buy—everything their little hearts desire—but they simply don't appreciate it. Maybe someday they'll be thankful. Well. I guess life has its difficulties, doesn't it. Here we are, now. This is where the Olsons live."

Mrs. Maxwell parked on the street and everyone climbed out.

"Allow me to help carry your things, Mrs. Clayton. Oh, dear, I forgot. I'm wearing my new heels. I'm so sorry. I'm sure you understand. I don't know why I chose these shoes this morning. I have half a dozen others to choose from, and I chose these. I suppose the thought just didn't cross my mind."

"Don't worry yourself, Mrs. Maxwell. There isn't that much anyway. The children and I can manage, I'm sure. Thank you."

"Anytime. I'll wait in the car and you come out when you're ready to go back to the station. Take your time. Only, I do have a Ladies Aid Society meeting in a few minutes. I really shouldn't be late since I'm the chairwoman. It's a very important meeting. But, as I said, don't rush." Again, Mrs. Maxwell's mouth stretched into a phony smile.

"Thank you," replied Mother shortly, trying to sound pleasant. "I won't be long."

Rhoda gripped Anna's hand like a vice. Her knees wobbled despite the late August heat as they stood in front of the Olsons' house.

"Don't be so nervous," Anna croaked hoarsely, trying to calm her own nerves in the process. "Mother wouldn't send us to just anybody's house. I'm sure the Olsons are very kind people. Besides, Mother said so. You don't think Mother would lie, do you?"

The laughter of Ruth and Elijah lightened the mood as the youngest Claytons skipped and hopped after being cooped up on their journey. Rhoda could picture Ruth's round, rosy face and jet black curls that she had inherited from Father. Elijah's chubby figure and shaggy blonde tresses flashed through her mind. Both had blue-green eyes, and Elijah's always seemed to bear a mischievous twinkle.

5

"Ain't you excited to meet the Olsons? What d'ya think they look like? I bet Mrs. Olson is real pretty, don't you think?" imagined Ruth. "And maybe Pastor Olson has a jolly laugh like Daddy had. Ya think so, Anna?"

"Silly, how can we know when we haven't even met 'em? You'll find out soon enough."

"Ith thith where we're gonna live 'til Charity getth better?" inquired Elijah in a small voice.

"Yes, Elijah," answered Mother, who was busy piling the luggage on the sidewalk.

"I can't wait ta see what their house is like inside," lilted Ruth.

It's easy for Ruth to be happy. She loves to meet new people. I wish I could go with Mother instead of staying here, Rhoda fumed to herself. Still, she was mildly curious.

"Tell me what it looks like, Ruth. Is it like our big farm house?" asked Rhoda, feeling a stab of sorrow that she could not see the Olsons' house for herself.

"It ain't like our house at all. It's a little smaller an' painted a nice shade of blue with petunias planted in front. There's a path leadin' up to the door an' a little porch with a pretty white rocking chair on it. An' there's a white fence around in the back yard. What could be back there? I can't wait to find out! It's so mysterious an' exciting!" Ruth finished melodramatically.

"Anna, please help me with the carpetbags. I can't carry them all myself," directed Mother. "Ruth, hold Rhoda's hand and be careful she doesn't trip on the porch steps. Come, Elijah."

Rhoda could envision Mother better than any other person. She clearly recalled her smooth, delicate face. Mother's eyes were a bold blue, and her demeanor was soft and inviting. Mother never wore her hair down, but modestly tucked her golden locks into a small bun to be kept out of the way while she tended to her daily chores.

6

Mother adjusted her felt cloche, and the small procession made their way up to the door of the house, which swung open before Mother had time to knock.

Ruth discretely described Mrs. Olson to Rhoda as they lingered a few steps behind. "She has such a nice smile an' a pretty face. She has orangeish-brownish hair that's short with puffy curls, an' she has on a plain blue dress that's neat an' clean. I wish you could see her, Rhoda."

Rhoda felt tears rise to her eyes. *I do, too.*

"Pauline, I'm so glad you've made it. Come in," beckoned Mrs. Olson cheerfully.

"Thank you so much for taking the children. You don't know what it means to me to know they're in good care," replied Mother.

"Nonsense. It'll be so good to have children in the house. I'm sorry my husband isn't here to greet you. He won't be back until this evening." She shifted her eyes toward the children. "Let me see, the tall one is Anna, right? It's hard to believe she's only thirteen. She looks so much older. I remember that silky, golden hair from when she was just a little thing, and I'm glad to see she hasn't outgrown those sweet dimples. And this is—"

"My name's Ruth, ma'am. I'm eight years old. An' this is Elijah. He's five an'—"

"Ruth, it's impolite to interrupt Mrs. Olson like that," Mother reminded gently.

"That's fine. She's simply eager, just as I have been." Mrs. Olson turned her attention to the gaunt form of a girl who had tucked herself behind her mother. Rhoda's formerly rosy appearance had not returned after her illness. Her dark floral-print dress contrasted sharply with her paleness. "And this must be Rhoda," Mrs. Olson continued delicately.

"Yes, ma'am," mumbled Rhoda, barely audible.

"Don't worry about any of them, Mrs. Clayton. We'll all have a wonderful time together while you're away. Will you be going right away, or might I persuade you to stay for some coffee?"

7

"Thank you, but I really need to be going if I want to make the train to Lakeview." Turning to the children, she kissed each one and bade them farewell, exhorting Elijah to try to keep out of mischief.

Mother pulled Rhoda close to her and whispered in her ear, "I promise to write when I get the chance and let you know how Charity's getting along. Be a good girl for Pastor and Mrs. Olson, won't you dear?"

"Yes, ma'am," Rhoda replied despondently.

"Thank you again, Rebecca," Mother said as she took Mrs. Olson's hand in both of her own and then turned to go.

"It's my pleasure. Please send my regards to your sister's family."

"Of course." Mother got into Lucille Maxwell's car, which soon rumbled to life and drove away.

Chapter Two:
The Ladies at Church

The Lord works in mysterious ways, marveled Rebecca Olson as the crew watched the car disappear around the corner. A conversation from only a few short weeks ago flashed through her mind.

♦   ♦   ♦

"Rebecca, it's so nice to hear your husband preach again. I've been gone for so long that it seems I've nearly forgotten what a wonderful treat it is to hear one of his sermons," crooned elderly Mrs. Bergs.

"It's good to see you back in church. I've missed you for the past few weeks," replied Rebecca. "I hope you're feeling much better. James and I have been praying for your quick recovery."

"Aren't you a sweetheart," said Mrs. Bergs, tenderly patting Rebecca's shoulder. "Yes, I'm feeling quite a bit better, but with this old body, rheumatism does take its toll. And how are you, Rebecca?"

"I've been quite well. I've been busy with my garden lately."

"Dear me, I've never seen a garden as beautiful as yours. You spend a lot of time on it, I suppose."

Out of the corner of her eye, Rebecca spotted another woman approaching. She groaned inwardly. *Not Lucille Maxwell.* Lucille was always spilling complaints and gossip wherever she went. Her shiny brown finger-waved hair was always neatly done and topped with the most fashionable millinery, and her turned-up nose enhanced her prideful countenance. Lucille had the unique ability to remind everyone of the things they wished to forget. Rebecca was one of her most commonly-chosen targets.

"How are you, ladies? Fine, I'm sure." Lucille sighed. "I'm as well as I can be when one takes into consideration all of my troubles. Sometimes, I just don't know where to start in telling of them."

"I hope it's nothing serious," Rebecca halfheartedly commented. "Are the boys doing alright?"

"Oh, that's the very subject, Rebecca, the very subject of my discomfort. You see, yesterday I went shopping, and do you know what those little rogues did? They locked Walter out of the house and ruined my new coat! Why, when I came home, it was practically in shreds." Lucille clicked her tongue. "I can imagine how clean and tidy one's home must seem when they don't have any children to tear it apart."

Lucille's words tore Rebecca's heart. Lucille was very aware of Rebecca's great desire to have children of her own. *I'd be satisfied with having the messiest house in the world if only I had children.*

The moment Lucille finally paused to take a breath, Rebecca excused herself and hurried toward the door. Stepping into the sunshine, she briefly closed her eyes and prayed, *God, why me? Why can the likes of Lucille Maxwell, who hardly cares for her sons more than she does a bread crumb under the table, have children? Why can't I be the one with children and Lucille the one without? I don't understand.*

Chapter Three:
An Answer to Prayer

The day the letter came, Rebecca's heart had leapt with joy.

"James! James!" she shouted, which was an unusual activity for reserved Rebecca.

"I'm in the study! What is it, darling?" James called in alarm, knocking his fountain pen and a stack of papers to the floor as he rose abruptly from his desk.

"We received a letter from the Claytons," Rebecca explained, her face radiant with happiness.

Realizing that there was no actual emergency, James bent down to retrieve his belongings.

Oblivious, Rebecca repeated, "We got a letter from the Claytons."

"The Claytons?" James replied thoughtfully, crawling out from under his desk. "That name doesn't ring a bell."

"They only lived in town for a short while a few years back. Remember? Samuel was the milk man for Wilkes' Creamery. His wife was an accomplished seamstress. She's the one who always brought her two little ones along to my Thursday morning Bible study."

"Ah, yes. Of course. The Claytons. Now I remember." Still not understanding what the excitement was about, he inquired, "What did they say?"

"Not they, dear. Only she. Sadly, it seems that Samuel passed away a few years ago. Pauline said—oh, here, read it for yourself." Rebecca handed him a cream-colored envelope.

James put on his spectacles. Pulling out the letter, he began to read. Silence filled the room as Rebecca held her breath. James' brow was furrowed. He exhaled forcefully and looked up into the shining eyes of his wife. Slowly, his face softened, and a smile replaced the look of doubt. "I think it would be a fine idea, if you're sure you can manage."

That was enough for Rebecca. She threw her arms around her husband. "Thank you, James! You don't know what it means to me. I'm certain I can manage them just fine."

"Of course you can," said James, chuckling at his wife's zeal. "Why don't you go answer that letter."

Rebecca had never known such glee. After responding to the letter, she immediately set to work preparing the house for the children. She arranged the two spare cots in the attic for the girls: the smaller one for Anna and the larger one for Rhoda and Ruth to share. She washed the bed sheets from the small guestroom downstairs for little Elijah. In the midst of fluffing a pillow, Rebecca suddenly stood stone-still.

Suppose the children are too hard for me to handle? Suppose we don't get along at all? Suppose I won't be a good caregiver for them? As she continued to fret, the realization that everything would be done according to her Master's plan soon swept her worries away.

"Why are you worried, Rebecca Olson?" she scolded herself aloud. "You know that God will take care of everything. Besides, it's of no use getting all flustered. I'm sure everything will go just fine and we will have no trouble whatsoever."

Little did she know that the day of the Claytons' arrival would be like a dream come true...and a full-blown nightmare.

Chapter Four:
The Way It Was

A pair of dusty, bare feet dangled leisurely from a limb on their owner's favorite climbing tree. The girl's mop of orange curls shone almost golden in the sunlight that filtered through the leaves. A light breeze blew, tangling strands of the girl's hair into the surrounding twigs. Humming "Skip to My Lou" and carefully picking the petals off of a daisy, the sprightly girl seemed to be in her own little world.

"Charity! How many times do I have to call? Come here now!" shouted a woman's voice.

Charity jumped deftly to the ground. She streaked toward the voice, leaving her paradise behind to enjoy some other day. Charity knew that Mama hated to tell her to do something more than once, so the thought of her mother's displeasure persuaded her to run even faster.

"Next time, come the first time I call for you, please," admonished the woman.

"Sorry, Mama. I was—"

"Daydreaming again. I know," Mama finished.

Mama was a sturdy woman—a strong and useful farm wife. She almost always wore her roomy floral apron and, like her daughter, was always barefoot except when there was company. Her long, curly hair matched Charity's, although it was much more auburn in color. Mama squinted up toward the sun. "What am I going to do with my little dreamer?"

Charity grinned. Mama could scold her terribly if she wanted to, but nonetheless, her heart was as warm as the sunshine itself.

"What's that you got?" queried Charity, noticing an envelope in her hand. Growing excited, she continued, "A letter from Daddy?"

Ever since Arthur Turner had left last winter to find work, their home seemed lonely. Letters from Daddy were a treat. Lately, though, no letters had come. Every day, Charity peered into the mailbox, and every day for the past two months, she had found it empty. *Daddy must have found work, and he's too busy to write,* Charity always tried to convince herself.

"No, it's a letter from Aunt Pauline. Guess who's coming to visit."

"My cousins!" Charity squealed and proceeded to jump up and down, clapping her hands.

"Land sakes, child! Let's put that energy into getting the house prepared."

As Charity scrubbed the kitchen's hardwood floor with an old rag, her mind drifted back to last summer when her cousins had come for a long visit.

♦   ♦   ♦

"Look at what I found!" touted Charity, grabbing a clam shell out of the sand. It was no bigger than the tip of Charity's thumb, but the interior was full of irridescent colors. Rhoda, Anna, and Ruth galloped across the beach to see their cousin's find.

"Look at the rainbow inside!" exclaimed Ruth.

"It's so pretty," observed Rhoda. "Can I hold it?"

"May I," corrected Anna.

"Knock it off, Anna. What's the big deal? It means the same thing," Rhoda replied.

"I found it right here," explained Charity, pointing to a barely visible indent in the sand.

"Maybe we can find more," suggested Rhoda eagerly.

Anna, always the delegator, pointed in different directions as she instructed: "Charity, you and Rhoda look over there. Ruth and me will look over here."

Charity and Rhoda looked at each other, grinning broadly.

"Ruth and *I*," they corrected together before dissolving into giggles and scampering away in their assigned direction, leaving Anna speechless.

Without warning, Rhoda lurched forward and landed face-down in the sand. She glared back at the old, sand-filled bottle that had tripped her, but her irritation didn't last long.

"I found another one." Rhoda plucked the shell from beside the bottle. "It's pretty, but it ain't as nice as yours," she commented after inspecting it.

"I like it better than mine," countered Charity. "Let's switch."

"Mother doesn't even have jewelry as pretty as these," marveled Rhoda.

"That's it!" Adopting a glamorous accent and posing with one hand on her hip, Charity continued, "Let's make 'em into swanky necklaces."

"Yeah!" concurred Rhoda.

Racing back to the picnic blanket, they found a red-checked napkin and carefully wrapped their shells. They quietly set the bundle on top of the basket and hurried away so as not to interrupt their mothers who were busily discussing the latest news.

"We found two more shells, but they're broken," announced Ruth, strolling with Anna over to where Charity and Rhoda stood. She opened her hand and displayed their contributions.

"Look at 'em later," broke in a boy's voice behind them. "Let'th go play in the water."

"You go play. We're looking for more shells. We'll play later," Anna retorted.

"Whatcha got behind you?" questioned Ruth suspiciously.

"Play in the water or you get wet," Elijah stated smugly as he produced a sloshing bucket.

"Elijah Clayton, if you dump water on us, I'll tell on you!" warned Anna. "We told you already. We're not going to—"

That was as far as she got before Elijah emptied his bucket in one splash right down the front of her dress.

15

"ELIJAH!" Anna screeched, running after her little brother who was laughing and running toward the lake. It was hard to stay angry, though, on such a carefree day amidst the warm breeze and the squeal of the gulls.

Charity, Rhoda, and Ruth chased after them, and soon they were all swimming and splashing each other with the cold lake water.

"Bette, you wouldn't believe what happened to the neighbors," Aunt Pauline began later that evening as the girls sat around the kitchen table and watched her carefully drill holes through the shells.

"You don't mean the Browns," Bette gasped, stringing embroidery thread through the holes. "Are they still not getting by very easy?"

"It's worse now. The bank's giving them one more week in their house, and then they're going to put a foreclosure on it."

"Those poor people. How many children do they have? Was it five? All under the age of ten, too, if I remember. I can't imagine how difficult it must be."

"I gave them some of Ruth's old feedsack dresses that don't fit her anymore for the little ones. Bette, I don't know what I'm going to do now for earnings. You know that I rented the fields out to the Browns. I'll have to find someone else to rent the fields to now. And the animals…Mr. Brown always took care of Dot and Thelma—you know, our milk cows—and the chickens and Sam and Claude. Such a dear he was to help us with all that. I've got enough on my hands just to put food on the table, much less worry about the animals' welfare. I suppose they'll have to go soon, too. To tell you the truth, Bette, I don't even see that the horse team is of any good to us. We don't use the fields anymore, and the renter does the plowing. Besides, Sam and Claude are just too old for that kind of work. Still, those horses have been on our farm as long as we have. I sure would hate to see them go." Aunt Pauline grabbed another shell and continued, "I guess the only thing that's certain is change. We'll all just have to work a little harder. Maybe I'll have to take on more seamstress work, but there are only so many hours in a day. Don't think that I'm sorry that the Browns are leaving just for my own sake. I certainly do feel bad for our poor neighbors. They've lived next door to us for years. Mrs. Brown and I have become such good friends. Such kind people. It's so sad to see them go. Mrs. Brown said they were going to move in with her brother and his wife for a while."

"They aren't the ones over in Iowa, are they?"

"No, you're probably thinking of Mr. Brown's cousin and her husband. Did I tell you about that? They moved to Iowa because the work was poor up in…"

Charity crawled onto her daddy's lap and tried not to listen. It seemed as though everyone had some kind of sad story related to the stock market crash. It was just too overwhelming for an eleven-year-old. Daddy kissed Charity's nose and put his arm around Elijah, who was planted on his other knee and in the process of dissecting an old broken pocket watch he had found at the beach.

"Now, you decide fairly among yourselves who gets what," instructed Charity's mother, turning to the children as she finished the last necklace. "I don't want you to get into any arguments about whose necklace is whose when it comes time for your cousins to leave." She looked hard at Charity, which meant, *Don't take the best for yourself before asking if your cousins would rather have it.*

That night as she dressed for bed, Rhoda thought about the conversation Aunt Bette had with Mother. Times were hard for so many people, but being with her best friend in the world made the hardships seem less…well…hard.

"Are you gonna keep your necklace forever?" Rhoda asked Charity.

"Sure. Why?"

"Let's both keep 'em forever an' promise that things will always be like they are right now. Nothing will ever change. Promise?"

"I promise. Nothing will ever change!"

17

Chapter Five:
The Shocking Visit

"Charity Turner, you'll wear yourself out before they even get here. Stop running around like that and be patient!" Mama advised disapprovingly.

"But it's almost time for 'em ta come, ain't it, Mama? What are they taking so long for? Ya think they forgot?"

"I'm sure they'll be here any minute." Mama continued to pack sandwiches and apples into the picnic basket.

Charity slumped onto the living room couch and watched Mama scurry around the kitchen. Something bothered her about the expression Mama wore, however. It was the same look that was often on Mama's face as she read the headlines in the newspaper. It was the look she had just before Daddy left to find work. Charity knew that look very well. It was worry. What was Mama worried about? Mama had never seemed worried when she had company. In fact, spending time with friends and family was one of her favorite pastimes. Perplexed, Charity hardly heard the knocking at the door.

"Charity! I'm surprised that you aren't halfway out the door by now. Didn't you hear the knock?"

The girl streaked to the door at once. However, when she opened it, she was stunned by the sight. Instead of joy, deep grief clouded Aunt Pauline's face. Rhoda's eyes had a strange appearance that puzzled Charity. Anna, Ruth, and Elijah all seemed downcast. Even the air around them seemed to hang heavy with gloominess. What had happened? Charity stood with her mouth gaping, unsure of what to say. Mama's warm hands rested on Charity's shoulders.

"Come in, everyone. Pauline, I'm so sorry. I don't know how it could've happened so suddenly."

For the first time since Uncle Samuel had died, Charity saw tears appear in her aunt's eyes.

"I know, Bette. We weren't prepared for it either."

What's 'it'? Charity wondered. *Did somebody die or something? Was this why Mama seemed so worried?*

Mama hugged Aunt Pauline and led her into the kitchen.

"Children," began Bette calmly, "I packed you a picnic lunch. Why don't you take the basket to the field with Charity. I want to talk to your mother now."

Charity was relieved to see some excitement light up her cousins' faces—all except for Rhoda's. Rhoda neither spoke nor looked at anyone. She seemed to be staring off into space.

Charity took the picnic basket, grabbed Rhoda's hand, and bolted for the door in order to lead the way to their favorite spot for picnics—a grassy field that was filled with daisies in the summertime. Rhoda resisted, standing still and expressionless as Charity, in the midst of her enthusiasm, was jerked to a halt.

"C'mon, Rhoda. Why aren't you coming?" she questioned with a nervous laugh.

"Charity, you don't know yet that—" began Anna.

"That I'm blind!" Rhoda exploded fiercely.

Charity was stunned. Did she hear what she thought she'd just heard? No. Not Rhoda. Could her cousin really be blind? It couldn't be.

"I'm not coming with you," Rhoda continued mechanically. "I'm staying with Mother."

"Come on, Charity," urged Anna gently. "Rhoda's not coming."

Charity, still holding Rhoda's hand, remained fixed like a statue.

"Just go, Charity," Rhoda cut in softly with a catch in her voice.

Slowly, Charity released her grip on Rhoda's hand. Still studying Rhoda's face, Charity backed toward the door as if in a daze. As she passed the threshold, the bright sunshine didn't even bring her around.

"Is it true, Anna? Is it really true? Is Rhoda actually blind?" A knot of sorrow budded deep inside Charity.

"It's true," Ruth blurted. "Rhoda was real sick an' now she can't see. An' she's always grumpy."

"Ruth! Don't say that. How would you like it if you were blind? Mother told us to be extra kind to her so she doesn't feel left out. Mother said that she hoped a visit to you, Charity, would cheer her up." Anna's words dissolved into the air.

"Let'th go eat!" called Elijah from far ahead of the three girls.

"Yippee!" squealed Ruth, prancing ahead to catch up with her brother.

Charity lingered behind.

"Coming?" asked Anna kindly.

"Yeah," she responded dully.

All throughout the picnic, Charity was quiet. The rustle of leaves in the trees and the sweet melody of song birds did nothing to change the atmosphere. It wasn't the same without Rhoda. Even the meal Mama had packed seemed tasteless. Charity mentally chastised herself. She knew she was making the visit gloomy, but she was in such shock. She yearned to hear what Aunt Pauline was telling Mama back at home. An idea arose in her mind.

Clearing her throat and forcing a smile, Charity jumped up and suggested, "I know! Let's go back and play hide-and-seek. The chicken coop is home base."

With whoops of approval, the troop stuffed everything into the picnic basket and raced back through the field. Anna was "it" first. As Anna counted to twenty, Charity hid behind a bush beneath the partly-opened kitchen window. She strained her ears to hear the conversation inside.

Aunt Pauline's voice was shaky as she spoke in a muted tone. "Why did this have to happen to my Rhoda? God already took Samuel. Must He afflict Rhoda, too? All around us is such grief and despair, Bette. President Hoover speaks of a great depression. Great depression, indeed."

Charity managed to build up the courage to peek in through the window. The grownups' backs were turned, so Charity relaxed and didn't worry about being seen by them. Creeping around the corner to the living room window, she peered in. Her gaze landed on Rhoda who was sitting by herself in a chair, expressionless, facing straight ahead toward the window under which Charity crouched. Tears crawled down Rhoda's cheeks, making Charity's heart ache with sorrow. Why Rhoda? Why her best friend in the world?

Chapter Six:
Never the Same

Charity sat directly across from Rhoda at supper. She watched Aunt Pauline cut up Rhoda's meal and tell her where each food was located on her plate before seating herself. Rhoda only picked at her food. Her formerly healthy appetite had vanished.

"Rhoda? Tonight d'ya wanna read with me from the book Daddy gave me for my birthday last year? I can read out loud that funny story we both like best. I can describe what the pictures look like."

Rhoda didn't say anything at first, and Charity thought her offer had been declined. Presently, however, Rhoda nodded slightly.

Charity hoped that the stories would bring her best friend around to her usual self. The visit wasn't at all as it should be. Conversation was forced. It felt as if the two girls had never before met.

At bedtime, Charity and Rhoda sat in their nightgowns leaning against Charity's bed. Elijah had been asleep on the couch downstairs for some time. Ruth and Anna were unmoving lumps on the spare cot in the corner of Charity's bedroom. Charity held the book in her lap while the dim glow of the lantern fell on the page. As she read the words aloud, she stole an occasional peek at her friend. Rhoda seemed far off. She didn't smile even a hint at humorous parts in the story. After reading a full page, Charity closed the book.

"I'm sorry you can't read an' see the pictures," Charity said sympathetically after a long moment of silence. "I can't imagine what it's like ta be blind."

"I can't bear it. It's not at all like it used to be. Nothing will ever be the same."

Rhoda stumbled to her feet, cautiously groped her way into Charity's bed, and snuggled down under the covers. "Good night," she said, her voice muffled in the pillow.

"Good night," Charity repeated. She placed the book on the wooden shelf near her bed. Putting out the kerosene lantern that had shed a warm, comfortable glow in the bedroom, Charity felt her way in the cool darkness toward her makeshift bed on the floor.

Before crawling in, she tiptoed to her dresser. Tears bubbled into her own eyes now as she quietly felt around for her shell necklace. Picking it up, she pressed it to her aching heart. Rhoda's words echoed in her mind: "Nothing will ever be the same."

Chapter Seven:
The Trouble Begins

As soon as Lucille Maxwell's car had turned the corner at the end of the street, Elijah and Ruth sprinted through the open door of the Olsons' house and began to look around at all the curiosities. Ruth's attention was drawn to an end table, upon which sat a lamp with golden tassels hanging from the shade.

"What a pretty lamp! But," Ruth's brow furrowed, "how does it light up? Where does the kerosene go?"

"There isn't any kerosene for this lamp, Ruth. We have electric lamps in town. We don't have to light them. We just turn on a switch. Like this." Mrs. Olson reached under the shade and demonstrated.

Ruth's eyes grew wide with astonishment. Fascinated, she turned the switch, which turned the lamp off.

"Can I do it again, please?" begged Ruth.

"May I," corrected Anna.

"Of course. Come, Elijah, Rhoda. You come and try, too."

"No, thank you," replied, Rhoda with a frown. "I can't see the light anyway."

"Oh, I'm…I'm very sorry," sputtered Mrs. Olson. "I…" Mrs. Olson turned around. Elijah had disappeared. "Where did Elijah go?"

"I don't know. I thought he was here," replied Anna, looking around for the impish boy.

Then they heard it: the sound of running water. A knowing look crossed Mrs. Olson's face. "I know where he is."

When Rebecca entered the kitchen, she stared in horror at the water flowing out of the sink and splashing down onto the floor like Niagara Falls. Elijah was standing on a chair, holding his hands under the faucet, completely oblivious to the mess he was making. He appeared totally delighted with his discovery. Determined to make the children like her, Mrs. Olson refrained from saying anything about the mess.

"Ith thith your well, Mitheth Olthon?" Elijah inquired.

"That's our faucet. We use it like a well, only it's inside our house so we don't have to go outside to get our water." Mrs. Olson turned off the tap and lifted Elijah, soaking wet, to the floor.

"I like your houth. It thure ith fun ta play with!"

"I'm glad you think so, but I think we need to get you into some dry clothes."

As Mrs. Olson mopped up the water, Anna hurried in, dragging Rhoda behind her.

"I'm sorry about the mess, ma'am. Elijah didn't mean to. We don't have a…one of those things in our house. He's just excited."

"You girls come and see how it works, too."

Anna carefully pulled up the handle, and out poured the water. She put her hand under the stream.

"Rhoda, give me your hand and feel the water. The Olsons have indoor plumbing!"

"No, thank you," Rhoda again replied. She pulled away and stood with her arms crossed over her chest.

Anna turned off the water and helped Mrs. Olson mop up the rest of Elijah's mess.

Rebecca stopped and remained motionless for a moment. *Flussshhh. Flussshhh.*

From the next room, she heard Ruth declare, "My turn, Elijah. Let me have a turn!"

"Oh, dear. I think the little explorers have found something else to play with," Rebecca observed with an uneasy smile.

For fifteen minutes, she watched as the youngest Clayton children, who had never seen many modern appliances, raced about poking and prodding at anything unusual and begging to know how it worked. The sinks, lamps, toilet, and toaster had never been investigated so intently. Mrs. Olson kept her cool and didn't reprimand little Elijah for his unending ability to make messes. It seemed to her that Rhoda was just as interested as her siblings, even though she sulked in the corner and didn't respond when Mrs. Olson tried to talk to her. Finally, the children were satisfied with seeing all that sparked their curiosity, and Rebecca was able to get Elijah into dry clothes.

"Now, then," Mrs. Olson announced cheerily as she collected herself. "I suppose I should show you where you are to sleep. Follow me."

Rebecca took Rhoda's hand. Rhoda hesitated until Anna firmly nudged her from behind. Leading the children down a hallway, Mrs. Olson showed Elijah to the guest bedroom.

"Hot diggity dog!" Elijah bounced around the room and flopped down on the bed. "Thith room hath a lamp with a thwitch, too!"

"Yes, it does. Put your things in the dresser, and I'll be right back."

Rhoda heard Mrs. Olson open a door at the end of the hall.

"I hope you can manage the stairs all right, dear. Here's the railing, and I'll make sure someone is always with you so that you don't—"

"I can manage," Rhoda interjected coldly.

Mrs. Olson didn't seem bothered by Rhoda's rudeness as she led the girls up the creaky wooden stairs. When they had reached the top, Rebecca explained, "That cot over there is for Ruth and Rhoda, and this cot is for Anna. You may all put your clothes in the dresser. I'll give you some time to unpack now. If you need anything, please let me know."

"Thank you very much," expressed Anna politely.

"Why don't I have my own bed like Elijah and Anna?" Rhoda demanded. "At home, I had my own bed."

Mrs. Olson seemed startled.

"Rhoda!" Anna rebuked in a coarse whisper, pulling her sister aside. "Stop being so rude. Mrs. Olson went to a lot of trouble for us, and maybe she wants to change her mind about taking us in after she's seen how rude you've been!"

"Of course not," assured Mrs. Olson. "I'm sure it's a big change when Rhoda's used to her own bed. I'm so sorry. We didn't have another spare cot."

"I'm happy that all of us get ta sleep in the same room," remarked Ruth, who always tried to look on the bright side of situations.

"I'm glad. I tried to make it as comfortable as I could. Now I'd better go help Elijah. If you girls need anything, I'll either be in Elijah's room or in the kitchen preparing supper."

The second Mrs. Olson reached the bottom stair, Rhoda burst into tears.

"You're being very selfish," Anna fumed.

"I want my own bed, an' I don't wanna sleep in a smelly old attic," she whined, for it didn't take her long to match the faint musty smell with that of an attic. "I wanna go home. I don't wanna stay here with Mrs. Olson because I don't like her."

"Rhoda!" exploded Anna and Ruth together.

"She called me 'dear.' I'm not her 'dear.' That's what Mother calls me."

"Would you rather she called you 'pickle-face'?" put in Ruth. "Mrs. Olson is nice."

"Hurry and put away your things, Ruth. You and I need to help Mrs. Olson get supper ready," Anna directed. "We need to earn our keep here," she added emphatically with her eyes set on Rhoda.

"What will I do? There's nothing for me to do here. It's such a dull house," Rhoda complained.

"You can stay here and think about how terribly you've behaved," responded Anna in an icy tone. "You should be ashamed of yourself," she called back as she headed down the stairs.

Ruth helped Rhoda put her things away and tried to cheer her up.

27

"I know. I'll ask Mrs. Olson right after supper if we can go out into her garden. I saw it through the kitchen window. I bet it smells real good. We could sit there an' smell the flowers an' I can tell you all about everything. That'll make you happy again."

Rhoda pressed her lips together and turned away. Ruth gave up and followed Anna downstairs, leaving Rhoda all alone in the small attic room.

Nothing can ever make me happy. Rhoda sat on her cot, intent on remaining angry and miserable. Her thoughts wandered to Mother and then to Mrs. Olson. She soon began to feel sorry for the way she had spoken. *I promised Mother I'd be good. Mrs. Olson will tell her all about how awful I've been, and she'll be horribly disappointed with me.* At that moment, she heard Mrs. Olson's voice from downstairs.

"Rhoda, come here, please."

Rhoda knew she was going to be punished for her bad attitude. What would Mrs. Olson do? Would she send her away? Rhoda tried to shove that thought out of her mind. She slowly descended the stairs, a feeling of dread increasing with every step.

Chapter Eight:
Pastor Olson

Rhoda shivered like a frightened kitten on the bottom stair and braced herself for punishment. Mrs. Olson led her down the hall without a word.

"Pastor Olson is home now," Mrs. Olson stated simply as they reached the kitchen.

"Hello, Rhoda. Glad to meet you," rumbled a strong and friendly voice.

Rhoda squeaked a "glad-to-meet-you-sir" in return and continued to shift uneasily.

Mrs. Olson led her to the sink where Rhoda washed her hands before being guided to the table.

"Anna, would you mind filling the water glasses while I give those mashed potatoes a stir?"

"Yes, ma'am," Anna responded cheerfully. The kitchen was one of her favorite places to be.

"Lemme do it, Anna!" shouted Elijah, hurrying over to the sink to turn on the water.

"James, how are the Petersons getting along?" Mrs. Olson inquired as she lifted the lid of the pot. Steam wafted up in a giant puff.

Pastor Olson briefly described his visit with Wayne and Eileen Peterson, an elderly couple with whom the Olsons had been friends for many years. They had recently moved off their farm to a home in a neighboring town.

Rhoda was dumbfounded. Where was her punishment? Had Mrs. Olson decided to ignore Rhoda's bad behavior?

Pastor Olson ambled toward the sink to clean the day's grime off his hands.

Just as Pastor Olson touched the faucet handle, Elijah begged, "Can I do it pleathe, thir?"

29

"May I," corrected Anna.

"No, Anna, I wanna. I athked firtht."

Pastor Olson winked at Anna and then turned to Elijah. "Absolutely! I always like to see an eager helper."

"Well, aren't ya gonna describe what he looks like?" hissed Rhoda crossly as she leaned toward Ruth.

Ruth whispered back, "Pastor Olson has brown eyes and really dark brown hair that's all nice and smoothed back. He's even taller than Mr. Brown!"

"Supper time!" Mrs. Olson sang.

"I'm sure not opposed to that," Pastor Olson declared while plunking into a chair next to Elijah. After carving the roast into thin slices, he bowed his head and closed his eyes.

"Pathtor Olthon, are you goin' ta thleep before eatin' thupper?"

"I'm not going to sleep, Elijah," Pastor Olson explained. "I'm going to pray to God and thank Him for our food."

"But why're you clothing yer eyeth?"

"Closing my eyes helps me to think about what I'm saying when I pray."

"I'm gonna clothe my eyeth, too. But I ain't fallin' athleep. I'm jutht thinkin', like you."

Rhoda's stomach growled as Pastor Olson prayed. She wished he would hurry up and finish so she could eat, but then the realization hit that her food had not been cut up. Stubbornly, she crossed her arms and leaned back in her chair. Anna kicked Rhoda under the table. Rhoda kicked her in return and clenched her teeth.

Finally, Mrs. Olson cleared her throat and asked, "Why aren't you eating, Rhoda?"

"I don't know where anything is on my plate. Mother always tells me." She added plainly, "And you didn't cut it up for me."

Pastor Olson raised an eyebrow toward Mrs. Olson as he wiped his mouth with a napkin.

"I should've known," Mrs. Olson replied apologetically. "I'm so sorry, Rhoda, dear."

Stop calling me that! Rhoda seethed inwardly.

After cutting up Rhoda's meat and showing her where everything was located, Mrs. Olson returned to her seat.

Rhoda could hear Elijah, sitting at her right, stuffing himself. "Pathtor Olthon, will my couthin Charity die like my daddy did?" he asked with his mouth full of green beans.

"Sir, you'll have to excuse Elijah," Anna said quickly. "You see, Daddy died in a farm accident when Elijah was only a year old, an' now he asks if everyone's gonna die."

Rhoda swallowed hard. The question had been on the tip of her tongue since she'd heard that Charity was sick. She awaited Pastor Olson's response.

"Well, now. I can't exactly know the answer to that good question, young man. Some people do die if they're very sick. You've been sick before, haven't you?"

"Yeth, thir. Me and Ruth got the chickenpockth. We itched real bad on account o' the thpots. Thometimth I took a dinner fork ta itch the thpots I couldn't quite reach, like the ones on my—"

"Elijah," Anna broke in. "That is not proper dinner conversation."

Unfazed, and finding himself becoming quite fond of the boy, Pastor Olson continued, "But you don't have the chickenpox now."

"No, thir."

"That's because God decided to make you better. If God decides to make Charity better, then she will get better. You see, God is in control of everything."

Rhoda took a bite of her potatoes and pretended not to be interested.

"An' what if God don't want her t' git better?" Elijah probed.

Mrs. Olson cast an anxious glance toward her husband and interrupted brightly, "Who wants a treat? I made cookies to celebrate your arrival."

"Hot diggity dog! Cookieth!" Elijah exclaimed, forgetting his question.

31

Following the meal, Anna, Ruth, and Mrs. Olson cleared the dishes from the table while Elijah helped Pastor Olson fill the sink with sudsy dishwater. Rhoda sat at the table with her chin resting in her hands. She glowered while she listened to the clanking of dinnerware and the lively conversation.

"Mrs. Olson, I noticed that you have a garden in back of your house."

"Yes, I do, Ruth. Gardening is one of my hobbies."

"Can we go out an' see it?" Ruth asked.

"May we go and see it," corrected Anna. "And, no, we may not. We need to help Pastor and Mrs. Olson with the dishes."

"Oh, don't you worry about the dishes. I'll see to them. You all go on and play outside for a while. It's such a beautiful evening."

"Yay!" Ruth dashed out the door, followed by Elijah who was still clutching his sopping wet dish cloth. He left a trail of soapy water across the kitchen floor.

"Elijah!" gasped Anna. "You're dripping water all over the place! Put that back in the sink."

"Oopth," replied Elijah, starting back toward the sink.

"I don't want you to slip and fall," cautioned Mrs. Olson. "Toss it to Pastor Olson, and then you run along outside to play, okay?"

"Okay," agreed Elijah. After making a surprisingly accurate, albeit sloppy, toss to Pastor Olson, Elijah raced out the door to catch up with Ruth.

Anna remembered to thank the Olsons before grabbing Rhoda's hand. Before she could protest, Rhoda was dragged out the back door, as well.

Upon hearing the screen door slam shut, James burst into a robust laugh.

Rebecca let out her breath as she began to scrub the dishes. She hadn't realized she'd been holding it.

"That boy's gonna keep me in stitches," James commented as he wiped his eyes and grabbed a mop to clean up the mess. "Has everything gone alright?"

Rebecca chuckled. "I'm just a little worn out. It's too bad you weren't here when the children first came. They were fascinated with some of the modern furnishing in the house. Elijah especially fancies the indoor plumbing."

"I gathered that," replied James.

"Elijah is such a sweet little boy, but I've been chasing him all over the house trying to prevent him from making any more messes!"

James chortled as Rebecca relayed Elijah's antics. "I wish I'd have been here to see it all. Tell me about the others."

"Anna is a darling young lady," Rebecca continued, "and Ruth has a heart of gold. I know I'll really enjoy having children in the house. I love them all already. I'm just worried about precious Rhoda. I'm not really sure how to reach her. I know she doesn't want to be here. She's been sullen all day. I feel so bad for that poor girl, and I want so much for her to like me. I just don't quite know what to do. I guess maybe she just needs a little more time to adjust. It is only their first day here, after all. It must be hard for them— the poor dears."

"You'll do just fine, darling. I'm convinced of it," Pastor Olson reassured her, sauntering over to plant a kiss on her forehead.

"I sure hope so," Mrs. Olson responded uncertainly.

Chapter Nine:
Thirsty For Money

The frail woman hunched her shoulders and pulled her well-worn shawl closer around her scrawny body, even though the thermometer read 85 degrees. Her eyes remained fixed on the ground as she tripped along at a pace surprisingly quick for her figure. A closer look would have revealed stringy gray hair peeking out from under her light green scarf and a face wrinkled not so much by age as by hard living. Men's loafers adorned her feet. They were bursting at the seams, revealing newspaper and cardboard stuffed in the bottoms. People strolling by stared as she made her way along. Some clutched their belongings more tightly, knowing that the homeless had reason—and reputation—to steal.

Elegance, status, and wealth had all abandoned the woman three years ago. Nineteen twenty-nine would forever be seared in her memory. That fateful year, the economic crash had claimed her former lifestyle forever. No longer was she "Miss Louise Harris," the heiress, but she was now known as "Beggar Harris."

During her years of living in a Hooverville just outside of Briggsville, Louise had conformed to the ways of many other vagrants. In fact, she had been involved in quite a few petty thefts in order to make ends meet. At first, she had been bothered by her own actions, but it didn't take long for her conscience to die and for her heart to become as cold as the money she had once possessed.

Louise made her way out of town and strode into the hovel she called home. One unfamiliar with the conditions of such a place might have been horrified, but to Louise's calloused eyes, she was simply walking through a commonplace neighborhood.

Ramshackle houses composed of odds-and-ends, along with worn, homemade tents, made up the small town. Some residents, dressed in rags, stirred a pot of mulligan stew made from scraps of food that the homeless had gathered. Others hung up clothes on a tree branch that served as a sturdy clothesline.

Louise reached under her shawl and pulled out a wilted carrot and two wrinkled potatoes to contribute to the stew. The rule was simple: If you don't contribute, you don't eat. It was a very motivating rule if one wanted dinner.

Louise seated herself near the fire above which the soup pot hung. She set to work peeling and chopping her produce with the rusty pocket knife that was one of her scant possessions. Talk around the fire was livelier than it had been in a while because Tom Jennings had stolen a whole turkey for the stew that day. The aroma was heavenly.

"Got it right in broad daylight," he announced proudly to anyone who happened to be listening, "an' no one ever even missed it." As Tom continued to boast of his conquest, Dorothy Wendell plopped down beside Louise.

"Where'd ya get the carrot 'n taters?" she asked hungrily.

"Mind your own beeswax, and go away while you're at it. If I say something out loud, someone's gonna go and run me outta business."

"You mean someone hired you to work in exchange for the veggies? Where do they live?"

"Like I said, mind your own beeswax," lashed Louise with a glare. She knew that Dorothy hadn't been able to contribute to the stew, so she would go hungry again. Although it seemed harsh, survival of the fittest was the name of the game.

Dorothy got up in a huff. "I don't know why I even waste my breath talking to you."

"Me neither. You might get some stew if you'd actually work for it," Louise shot after her.

Dorothy was known to sit around in the Hooverville, staring off into space or sleeping. A deep depression often racked her—a response to the hard blows life had dealt her.

Both of her little girls and her fourteen-year-old boy had died of starvation and disease, and she didn't seem far behind. She refused to steal her food and often went hungry because of it.

Louise didn't feel sorry for what she'd said. "What that woman needs is a kick outta town," she grumbled under her breath.

Louise recalled how she, herself, had been kicked out of town when she could no longer pay her debts. Because of her love for money and uppity attitude toward others, her relatives had all turned their backs on her when she was in need, thus giving her no choice but to leave her home to find sustenance. The spite she had felt that when her world collapsed returned to her now. Beggar Harris. That title hurt her more than the pangs of hunger she often felt.

As Louise continued to chop her vegetables by the fire, she tried to forget the insults with which she had been hammered, but her hatred continued to grow until it was almost volcanic.

"I'll show 'em I'm no beggar. I'll be 'Miss Louise Harris' again if it's the last thing I ever set my mind on."

Chapter Ten:
The Stranger

As the ragtag residents of the Hooverville devoured the mulligan stew, a man not unlike them approached. His plaid shirt and overalls showed much wear, and he was badly in need of a shave. He might have been mistaken for one of their own except for the way he crept cautiously by, carrying his bindle and looking as though he wasn't quite sure where to go. Everyone watched until a few of the men stopped him and asked what he wanted. His explanation was a sadly familiar one.

"I've got a family back home," he explained, "and we're short on money."

Before he could continue, Ronald, a hobo with a scraggly grey beard and a significantly hunched back broke in, "Well, y' came ta the wrong place. You won't find any money in this dive."

This drew some snickers and hoots from his audience.

The man hesitated, scanned the faces of those assembled, and continued. "I came to find work. For a long time now I been lookin' for a good job, but there ain't one to be had. I been ridin' the rails, and it's the same story everywhere: no work. The little money I had I gambled away in hopes of gainin' enough to put food on the table back home, but I lost everything." The man's chin trembled. "I...I can't bear to face my wife and little girl. I can't bear to see the looks on their faces when I go home empty-handed. I can't go home, but I got nowhere else to go. I...I..."

"Well, it ain't the Ritz, but yer welcome ta stay," offered Ronald. "We eat whatever we can git. Put it into a community pot, usually. See if ya can git some kinda odd job day-by-day or learn to steal without gittin' caught. Build yerself a shelter with whatever junk you can scrounge up," he advised.

"Thank you, sir." Relief washed over the man's tired body.

"What do they call you?"

The newcomer hesitated for a moment. "Call me Samuel...Samuel Decker."

The stranger's reluctance amused the others. Samuel Decker, hey? Not likely. However, the man had spoken, and everyone called him Sam.

Sam proved himself useful around the camp. He was a hard worker with strong muscles and leathery skin that attested to the years he had spent as a farmer laboring in the sun. Because of his hardy work ethic, he was generally able to find small odd jobs and almost never failed to contribute to the stew. Even Louise admired his strength and practicality. Still, she sensed a shiftiness in his character.

This Samuel Decker fella just might come in handy to me some day.

Chapter Eleven:
Day Two

Saturday was work day. Laundry, baking, and cleaning all had to be done by bedtime.

"May I be in charge of the baking today?" pleaded Anna.

"Of course. That would be a big help to me. Two loaves of bread will do. I was planning to make an apple pie for tomorrow, too. But first, would you please collect the dirty laundry in the basket upstairs?"

"Yes, ma'am," Anna replied, hurrying to follow her instruction.

"What about me?" asked Ruth eagerly. "What can I do?"

"Would you like to wash the clothes that Anna brings down? The small wringer washtub is in the closet, but I'll set it up outside by the clothesline for you. I think Rhoda might even be able to help. I'm sure she can turn the crank or scrub the clothes on the washboard. Then you can hang the clothes up on the line."

"Yes, ma'am! I like washin' clothes," replied Ruth, loping off to find Rhoda.

While Rebecca washed the brunch dishes, James tried to finish his sermon—a difficult task with a fascinated youngster running around the study asking an unending stream of questions.

"What'th thith book about?" asked Elijah, hefting a thick volume from one of the shelves that lined the wall.

"That's a commentary on the book of Daniel," Pastor Olson explained, looking up briefly from his sermon outline.

"What'th a commentary? Who'th Daniel? Hey, what'th that in the drawer?"

Pastor Olson chuckled to himself, despite his frustration, as Elijah continued to poke around the study.

Mrs. Olson popped her head in and called, "Come here, Elijah, and help me with the dishes, please."

Elijah crawled out from under Pastor Olson's desk and wandered into the kitchen.

After he was out of earshot, Rebecca assured her husband, "I'll try to keep him busy so you can finish your sermon, dear."

James shook his head and chuckled again. "I'm sure there's a sermon illustration somewhere in all this."

A knock at the front door interrupted the conversation.

"I wonder who that is," Rebecca remarked as she hurried to greet the visitor.

"Good day, Rebecca," Lucille Maxwell hailed in an airy tone.

"Hello, Lucille," Rebecca replied, straightening her apron.

"I came by to see if that little boy—Elijah, is it?— would like to play with Dick and Andrew today. And, of course, I was wondering how you're all getting along?" Mrs. Maxwell ended in a questioning tone.

"Everything's fine," Mrs. Olson said hastily. "Elijah, would you like to play with the Maxwell boys today?"

"Coming!" shouted Elijah enthusiastically.

Crash!

Rebecca and Lucille hurried into the kitchen. The smashed remains of a plate lay scattered on the hardwood floor with Elijah in the midst of it.

"Are you alright?" Mrs. Olson asked, brushing broken ceramic off of his trousers.

"Yeth. I'm thorry, Mitheth Olthon. I wrecked yer purdy plate. Them thingth thure are thlippery when they're all wet!"

While Elijah and Rebecca picked up the pieces, Lucille stood scrutinizing the spectacle.

"I'll paste it back together, Mitheth Olthon," offered Elijah.

"No, we'll just throw the pieces out. We have more plates. I know you didn't mean to drop it. It's only a plate. I'm glad you're okay."

Elijah flashed a grin that displayed his missing front teeth, threw his arms around Rebecca's neck, and resumed picking up the pieces.

Rebecca's heart melted.

Ruth appeared at the kitchen door, pulling Rhoda along behind her.

"She says she won't do it 'cause she don't know how," Ruth explained after greeting Mrs. Maxwell.

"What's that, Ruth? Oh. Don't worry, Rhoda. I'll help you with the wringer in a minute," Mrs. Olson assured her.

"But she knowth how," interjected Elijah. "She jutht don't wanna."

"Dick and Andrew are waiting for you outside, Elijah," Mrs. Maxwell said in a tone that caused the boy to dash out as quickly as he could.

"We'll wait for you outside by the clothesline, Mrs. Olson," Ruth declared as she hurried after her brother, Rhoda in tow.

"Honestly, Rebecca, I don't think you have it in you to be a mother," Mrs. Maxwell said after the children had gone. "I don't mean to offend you, of course, but you really must learn how to discipline that boy! Why, if that were Andrew or Dick...." Lucille clucked her tongue.

"Well," Rebecca responded slowly, "it was just an accident."

"An accident, indeed!" retorted Lucille. "And that rebellious girl. She needs to do as she's told, blind or not. But if you don't want to listen to the suggestion of an experienced mother, then I'll just go home. I'll be back for Dick and Andrew at six o'clock."

With that, Lucille took one last disgusted look at the shards on the floor and marched out, slamming the door behind her.

Anna strolled in with the basket of laundry in her arms. "Here are the clothes, ma'am. Would you like me to take them outside to Ruth and Rhoda?"

41

When Mrs. Olson didn't respond, Anna repeated her question.

"Oh, yes. I'm sorry, Anna. Yes, please take the basket out to the girls."

As soon as Anna had shut the door, Mrs. Olson collapsed in a kitchen chair and sighed heavily. *Is Lucille Maxwell capable of saying just one kind thing? Just one?* Fear of failure crept into her mind. *Maybe Lucille is right....No, I know that it was just an accident. Elijah was only trying to help.*

Brushing away the hurtful remarks as best as she could, Mrs. Olson rolled up her sleeves and began to scrub the floor.

Anna soon returned and dumped a cup of flour into a bowl. "Thank you for letting me bake. I'm always in charge of the baking at home because I like to bake so much. Ruth helps Mother with the cleaning, and Elijah mostly just runs around underfoot."

"And what does Rhoda do to help?" inquired Mrs. Olson.

"Well, not really anything, I guess. She complains so much that Mother would rather do Rhoda's share of the work than put up with her fussing. I think Rhoda doesn't like to work because she can't see anything."

"What does Rhoda do instead?" Mrs. Olson asked.

Before Anna could answer her, the door burst open and Ruth tumbled in.

"Mrs. Olson! Rhoda dumped the wash water on me!"

"Why did she do that?" Mrs. Olson asked, stuffing her rag into the bucket and placing a hand on the wet girl's cheek. "Let's get you into a dry frock, and then you tell me what happened."

"I'll fill the washtub back up, ma'am," offered Anna.

"Thank you, Anna. Bring Rhoda inside, too, please."

Before long, Ruth was in dry clothes, and Mrs. Olson listened to her story.

"Anna told Rhoda ta wash the clothes ta earn her keep. She scrubbed the clothes on the washboard, but she wasn't scrubbing 'em hard enough ta get 'em good an' clean. I tried

42

ta tell her, but she wouldn't listen ta me. Then I took the clothes an' showed her how ta do it right, an' she got angry an' said that I don't know nothin'. Then she tipped the washtub over on me."

"Here she is, ma'am," Anna announced, gripping Rhoda's hand tightly so she wouldn't escape.

"Thank you, Anna. You may go back to your bread. Ruth, you run along and get the clothes washed. Rhoda, come here please."

Rhoda remained rooted to the floor. Rebecca stood her ground.

Following a short standoff, Rhoda shuffled closer.

"I'm very disappointed that you didn't control yourself when you felt angry. What you did was wrong. I'm going to have to punish you by sending you to your room."

Rhoda frowned. "Ain't ya gonna punish Ruth, too? She wouldn't let me wash the clothes by myself."

"I want you to go to your room now, Rhoda," Mrs. Olson instructed firmly.

"I can't find my way. I'm blind, remember?" Rhoda blurted impudently.

Without a word, Mrs. Olson led Rhoda to the attic stairs and watched as she ascended them.

After two hours, Ruth brought the empty clothes basket onto the porch where Rebecca was beating rugs.

"I'm done with the clothes, Mrs. Olson. D'ya want me ta do anything else?"

"No, not right now. You may play."

"Thank you. Can Rhoda an' me go in your garden?"

"May," Anna corrected from the kitchen, "and I."

"Of course," Mrs. Olson replied after a moment of thought. "I think Rhoda's been punished long enough. You may go and get her. She's upstairs."

Soon, Ruth was skipping around the garden. She picked rich purple sedums, delicate bluish-lavender hydrangeas, and a rainbow of dahlias.

"They're so beautiful! Feel the soft petals on the dahlias. An' the leaves on this one are so nice and thick."

Rhoda seemed to cheer up a bit as Ruth took her on a tour of the garden.

"I like the late summer flowers better than the early summer ones!" Ruth cried in delight.

"You always say you like early summer flowers better when they're the ones in bloom."

"I guess I like 'em all. Mrs. Olson has such a pretty garden. I'm gonna surprise her with a bouquet."

Before long, Rhoda heard a car pull up.

"It's that Mrs. Maxwell," Ruth said with obvious distaste as she peered through a crack in the fence. "Let's go inside and give Mrs. Olson her flowers."

Entering the kitchen, the girls could already hear Mrs. Maxwell's shrill voice.

"...and we'll be having guests for dinner," she was saying. "I thought I'd better come early for the boys so they may wash their hands and run a comb through their hair before our guests arrive."

"I'll call them in right now. They're still outside somewhere."

As she opened the door and called the boys' names, Ruth brought her hand out from behind her back and thrust a bouquet into Mrs. Olson's unsuspecting arms.

"I picked 'em for you. Surprise!" Ruth announced, beaming.

"Why, how sweet of you!" Rebecca smelled the bouquet and put her arm around Ruth's shoulders. "Let's put them in a vase on the table."

Lucille gasped in horror at the sight of the bouquet. "Rebecca! Your prized flowers! And you allowed these children to pick them? What are you going to enter in the fall flower competition?"

"Mrs. Olson?" Ruth turned inquiring eyes, brimming with moisture.

"I didn't pick any," Rhoda stated flatly.

44

"I think these flowers are right where they belong," consoled Rebecca, touched by the gift.

"I didn't know you were gonna put 'em in a competition. I never woulda picked 'em if I'da known they weren't fer pickin'," Ruth apologized, wiping her eyes.

"Don't cry. I like them much better on the table where they can brighten up the kitchen. I'm very glad you picked them for me. What a wonderful surprise! You may both pick as many as you want."

"As many as they want? Rebecca! It won't hurt the children to give them a scolding for ruining your flower garden. I just don't know what those children were thinking. They obviously have no idea that your flowers won first prize five years in a row. Why, whatever is everyone going to think? You always enter your flowers." Lowering her voice, Lucille added, "This is also going to reflect on your ability to handle the children. Oh, my. Well, I won't say a word to anyone. Not a word."

"I'd much rather have my flowers enjoyed by the children than entered in a frivolous competition."

"A frivolous compet—" was as far as Mrs. Maxwell got before she gasped again. Her hand flew to her mouth as three very dirty boys tumbled in through the door. "Oh! Oh! How...how could you let my boys get so filthy? Just look at them! They're completely covered in mud. Covered!"

"Rhoda dumped the wash water on Ruth an' it made a thwell mud puddle under the clothethline!" Elijah declared.

Lucille could only manage a small croak in response.

Rebecca was greatly humored as she realized this may have been the first time Lucille had ever been at a loss for words.

"Boys, into the car right now! I'm ashamed of you. Dirtying up your clothes like that. And with company arriving any minute! Rebecca, I hope you take my advice and take that boy on a trip to the wood shed. That's what he needs."

For the second time that day, Mrs. Maxwell slammed the door behind her.

"Doethn't Mitheth Maxwell like ta get jutht a little bit methy thometimeth?"

"No, I don't believe she does," Mrs. Olson replied, swallowing back a giggle. "Did you enjoy playing with Dick and Andrew?"

"We had oodleth o' fun. Andrew and Dick are thome pretty good eggth."

"I'm glad," Mrs. Olson said, tussling Elijah's fair, mud-encrusted locks.

Chapter Twelve:
Church

"Why, these must be the children I've heard so much about," Mrs. Bergs gushed.

"Good morning, Mrs. Bergs," greeted Rebecca. "I've been eager to introduce the children to you. This is Anna, the eldest of the four."

"How do you do, ma'am?" Anna courtsied.

"Now, let me get a good look at you. I believe I remember you from when you were just a little wisp of a thing. What's the last name?"

"Clayton," Anna replied. "Mother's name is Pauline and Father's name was Samuel."

"Yes, yes, that's right. I remember your mother and father. They weren't here very long, but I remember they had two precious little girls."

"This one is Rhoda," Rebecca continued.

When Rhoda didn't speak, Mrs. Bergs asked, "How do you do, Rhoda? You were just a little baby when—"

"Fine," Rhoda mumbled in response to Mrs. Bergs' question.

"That's nice," Mrs. Bergs replied graciously. "And the other two?"

"These are Ruth and Elijah," Rebecca replied.

"Such beautiful black curls you have, Ruth. You look so much like your father, doesn't she, Rebecca? Yes, I do remember the Claytons. And this is Elijah. You have the build of your father, young man."

Elijah beamed.

"Do I look thtrong?" He proudly displayed his muscles.

Mrs. Bergs patted his shoulder and answered, "Very strong. I'm sure you're a big help to your mother and the

47

Olsons. Oh, there's Gladys. I need to speak with her a moment. Please excuse me. It was so good to meet all of you."

"Let's go sit down. It's about time for church to start," Mrs. Olson explained.

"I get to sit by Mrs. Olson." Ruth plopped down next to the delighted woman.

"I wanna thit by Pathtor Olthon," Elijah said, becoming disappointed to find that Pastor Olson would not be sitting with them.

Mrs. Maxwell hastily approached and sat down. In a hushed, but emphatic, voice she complained, "These children aren't fit to be in church. The girls are wearing feedsacks, Rebecca. And the boy....His shirt and trousers are full of patches! To think, the pastor's wife, of all people, allowing such disrespect in God's house."

Pulling Elijah toward herself, Rebecca responded, "It seems to me that disrespect comes not so much from what one wears on the outside, but what one wears on the inside. Wouldn't you agree?" She smiled sweetly.

Mrs. Maxwell straightened up and answered brusquely, "Just the same, I am personally going to buy those children some decent church clothes. No, Rebecca, it wouldn't be any trouble at all," Mrs. Maxwell countered before Mrs. Olson could protest. "You cannot bring these children to church dressed in rags. I insist."

"Thank you, but that really will not be neces—"

"I'll go shopping first thing tomorrow morning. No need to worry. You needn't reimburse me. Being a banker's wife, it's not as if I can't afford it."

Mrs. Maxwell hurried off before Rebecca could say anything else.

"Good morning." Pastor Olson stood behind the pulpit.

"Hi, Pathtor Olthon!" called Elijah in response.

Some of the congregation snickered and murmured.

"Elijah, Pastor Olson has some important speaking to do now, so it's time to be quiet. Do you understand?" Mrs. Olson whispered softly.

"Yeth, ma'am."

Pastor Olson winked at the boy, who tried to wink back. He resorted to closing one eyelid with his pudgy finger. Pastor Olson had all he could do to keep himself composed.

"Before we begin, the Maxwells would like to make an announcement."

Lucille stood up, cleared her throat, and announced, "My husband and I have decided to open a soup kitchen at our expense. It will be in operation during the noon hour on Mondays, Wednesdays, and Fridays. If you'd like to serve as a volunteer, you may speak with me or my husband following the service. Vegetables and other contributions are welcome. Please know that this has been a desire of mine for a long time, and I look forward to seeing eager participation. It's the Christian thing to do, of course. I'd also like to ask on behalf of the Ladies Aid Society for volunteers to knit mittens and scarves for the homeless facing the harsh winter ahead."

"Thank you, Mrs. Maxwell. Now let's pray."

Rhoda soon tired of listening to Pastor Olson's sermon. She nudged Anna and whispered, "Is it almost over with? We never had to go to church before. Why do we have to now?"

"Why wouldn't we go to church if the people we're living with are the pastor and his wife? Just sit still and listen," Anna hissed in return.

Rhoda nudged Ruth's shoe with her own. "Ain't you tired of sittin' for so long?"

Ruth didn't answer for a moment. "I don't know what he's talking about," she finally muttered, "but it sure sounds nice what he's readin' from his book."

Rhoda listened to what Pastor Olson was saying.

"...The Lord is my shepherd; I shall not want. He maketh me to lie down in green pastures: he leadeth me beside the still waters..."

Just fluffy stuff. Ruth might like that kind of thing, but I don't, Rhoda thought to herself. Still, she decided to listen to a bit more of Pastor Olson's sermon.

"The verse we just read is one that you are all probably familiar with. It is another example of how the Bible compares us to sheep belonging to the Shepherd. It demonstrates how much God truly cares for us."

That was enough for Rhoda. She wanted nothing to do with that God who had made her blind.

For the remainder of the sermon, Rhoda blocked out every word Pastor Olson spoke.

Chapter Thirteen:
Aunt Pauline Comes

The raindrops skating down the windowpanes could not have been met with a more dismal sight. Inside the country farmhouse, a girl pale as chalk, yet with feverishly bright cheeks and lips, lay pathetically in her bed. A bowl of untouched soup on a table nearby proved that the invalid's appetite had failed. The girl's mother sat no more than a foot away, ready to do anything for the comfort of her daughter. Lips moving with earnest prayer and anxious glances cast longingly at the frail form added to the bleakness. Carefully-cut squares of fabric from worn-out clothes sat in the worried mother's lap, but her mind was far from the work that piled up in the sewing basket.

Mother and daughter were both unaware of the woman who made her way up to the front door. The lady carried a well-worn carpetbag in one hand and a small clutch purse in the other. Her hair was pulled up in its usual bun, and her calloused fingers were a sign of her diligent work habits.

A loud knock on the door immediately brought the mother to her feet. After a few brief words to the incoherent girl on the bed, she dashed to the door and threw it open.

"Pauline! Why, I didn't believe you would come, what with Rhoda needing you and all. I'm so worried."

"Bette, you're a wreck."

"I moved Charity's bed out to the living room where I could keep a closer eye on her. She's so weak." Bette broke down and began weeping, although she tried to smother her sobs. "It's been too long. I don't know how much more she can take."

Charity half-awoke from her fitful sleep and watched as Mama wrung her hands and talked with Aunt Pauline.

51

Mama, why is Aunt Pauline here? Charity voiced in her mind, but the words would not exit her mouth. Just as quickly as she had awakened, her thoughts became garbled and she again lost consciousness.

Charity tossed around beneath the seemingly thin blankets. She was vaguely aware that the women were there. Only bits and pieces of the conversation were audible.

"...scarlet fever..."

"... heard from him yet?"

"...hope he's not too late."

A sudden thought pierced Charity's fever-fogged brain. *Daddy? Am I really that sick that Mama hopes for Daddy to come home before it's...too late?* Chills, other than those from the fever, crept through every part of her body. *Am I going to die?*

Chapter Fourteen:
A Surprise

Sunday afternoon was a laid-back time for the Olsons and the Clayton children. Anna was sprawled out on the living room floor writing a poem in fancy lettering to give to Mrs. Olson as a surprise. Pastor Olson and Elijah were outside studying a turtle that Elijah had found next to the clothesline, and Mrs. Olson was teaching Ruth how to press flowers. Rhoda pretended to be asleep in the rocking chair.

"Go and find some heavy books that we can put on top of the newspaper, Ruth," instructed Mrs. Olson. "We need to put the other piece of newspaper on top of the flowers and stack books on them so they'll dry properly."

"Is this enough?" asked Ruth, cradling a large Bible and an unabridged dictionary in her arms.

"Plenty." Mrs. Olson positioned the books on top of the newspaper. "Now we'll wait for a few days, and when we take the books off, your flowers will be all done."

"Ain't they done now?" Ruth asked, staring at the piles of books on the kitchen counter. "Why do we need ta wait so long?"

"The flowers need the pressure to press out all the moisture in the petals. It takes a while to do that. Some things in life require lots of patience. If we take the books off now, the flowers won't be ready. They'll wither and rot, and you won't be able to enjoy them. But if we wait for them to be completely done, then you'll have beautiful flowers that'll last a long time. I'd say it's worth the wait, wouldn't you?"

Ruth nodded.

The door burst open, and Elijah ran in, followed by a panting, but delighted, Pastor Olson.

"The turtle crawled under the porch, and we can't thee it no more," Elijah announced. "It wath a purdy turtle, Mitheth Olthon. It had orange and green colorth on itth tummy!"

"A painted turtle," Pastor Olson explained.

"Did you touch that turtle?" asked Anna.

"And how!" Elijah replied radiantly. "I picked it up, an' then it put itth head an' armth an' legth inthide, an' all I could thee wath the thell! Pathtor Olthon thaid that it wath thcared of me, an' that'th why. D'ya think it wath thcared of me?"

"Yes, I think it probably was scared. I suppose it wasn't used to little boys picking it up," Mrs. Olson explained, giving his hair a tussle as she had become accustomed to doing.

"I dunno. Thomeone muthta picked 'im up ta paint the purdy colorth on hith tummy."

"No one painted the colors on that turtle, Elijah. He's called a painted turtle because it looks like someone painted the colors on him. That's how God made him."

"God painted the colorth on him?" asked Elijah thoughtfully.

"I suppose so," Mrs. Olson responded.

"I finished my poem," Anna announced, displaying her paper.

"My, how beautifully you've decorated it," Rebecca admired.

Anna smiled shyly. "I made if for you."

Rebecca was deeply moved as she accepted the gift and read the poem. "How thoughtful of you, Anna. I'll be sure to put it where everyone can see it."

"What can we do now?" Elijah asked.

"As a matter of fact, I have a little something for each of you," Pastor Olson answered mysteriously. "The day you arrived, I was visiting Mr. and Mrs. Peterson. They gave me some presents for you. I'll go and get them now, if you'd like."

"Oh!" squealed Ruth. "I wonder what they are."

James retrieved four small packages wrapped in brown paper. He handed them out to the children.

The wrapping on Elijah's was torn off in seconds. His eyes grew round as he held up an intricately-carved wooden steam engine. The wheels could turn, and coal was carved into the coal box.

"Hot diggity dog!" was all he could say.

"Look!" exclaimed Ruth. "It's a little box with a picture carved on it. And it's got my name carved on the top!"

"I have one, too," said Anna, "but with a different picture. See? Yours has a meadow with wildflowers and birds, and mine has trees by a brook."

"Mr. Peterson carved the train and the boxes himself," Pastor Olson stated. "He's an expert woodcarver."

"What did you get, Rhoda?" asked Rebecca, resting a hand on Rhoda's elbow.

Rhoda was carefully tracing with her fingers the smoothly carved design. Her voice was thin. "Lilies. Lilies and mountains."

Ruth peered over Rhoda's shoulder. "How pretty," she breathed. "Here's your name on the side."

Ruth held Rhoda's hand and traced her name for her.

A smile tugged at the corner of Rhoda's mouth. "I...I can see it all with...my fingers. It's so beautiful."

Pastor and Mrs. Olson exchanged hopeful glances.

"Wayne's carving is truly remarkable," agreed Pastor Olson.

"Did your friend really make these?" asked Ruth.

"Yes, he did," replied Mrs. Olson.

"I think we ought to do something nice for the Petersons," said Anna thoughtfully. "How 'bout we invite them over next Sunday! Ruth and I can do all the cooking, and Rhoda and Elijah can help in other ways. That is, if it's okay with you."

"That's very generous of you, Anna," Pastor Olson replied. "I think it's a fine idea."

"I think that would be wonderful!" Mrs. Olson agreed. "We'll talk about the details later. Right now, Anna, Ruth, we need to get your things ready for school tomorrow. Your teacher gave me a list of the things you need to bring. Rhoda, why don't you come and help."

Reluctantly, Rhoda followed her sisters into the kitchen to help them pack their book bags with the necessary items.

"Pathtor Olthon? Can you help me make trackth for my train?"

"Sure. I'll find some paste and scissors, and you ask Mrs. Olson for some pencils and newspaper."

The boys set to work drawing, cutting, and pasting. Elijah took the carved train and began to steer it wildly down the tracks that wrapped all around the study. Pastor Olson, who proved to be a child at heart, followed Elijah's train with a match box, using it as a makeshift locomotive. A whole lot of chugging and "woo woo"-ing drifted out from the room.

◆   ◆   ◆

The day drew to a close as everyone was involved in his or her own quiet activity. However, all activities stopped when Pastor Olson suggested, "Let's pray for your mother and Charity."

Joining hands, the group bowed their heads.

"Would anyone like to add anything?" Pastor Olson asked after he had finished.

Rhoda scowled in reply.

After the prayer, Ruth and Elijah seemed quieter than usual. Elijah lay down on the floor and drew circles with his finger on the rug. Ruth snuggled up into Mrs. Olson's lap. She wore a look that conveyed, *I miss Mother.*

Mrs. Olson, guessing why the sudden change had come over the two younger Claytons, hinted to her husband, "Maybe Pastor Olson has a story to tell us."

"Yes, I think I do. I have some really nice stories to tell you about people with your very own names."

"Ooh! Stories!" cried Ruth.

Pastor Olson settled himself into his armchair and motioned to Elijah, who scampered onto his lap. Ruth plopped down at Pastor Olson's feet, and even Anna, who was seated on the floor embroidering, put down her work and seemed eager to listen.

"Rhoda?" Mrs. Olson urged from her rocking chair.

"No, thank you. I'm tired," Rhoda grumbled as she proceeded methodically down the hall to the attic door.

Rhoda could hear Pastor Olson's strong, clear voice. She lingered just a minute at the end of the hallway to hear the beginning of Pastor Olson's story.

"This story is a true story from the Bible about a young lady named Ruth."

Hmph, sniffed Rhoda as she climbed the stairs to the attic room. She brought out the trinket box which she had carefully tucked away under her clothes in the dresser. Opening it, she pulled out her shell necklace. As her fingers touched the glassy interior, she began to worry anew about her cousin, and she longed for Mother.

Rhoda tried to ignore the exclamations of excitement that drifted up from the living room, but she ended up sitting at the top of the stairs, straining to hear parts of the stories about loyal Ruth and obedient Elijah. Why was she in a drab attic all by herself? She wished she'd stayed.

Chapter Fifteen:
News

The ragged bunch closed the makeshift church service with an a cappella verse of "It is Well with My Soul."

Louise Harris never attended the Hooverville church services that were held on Sunday mornings, but she always gathered with everyone afterward to hear the latest rumble. A large group gathered today, including Sam.

Frank got the ball rolling. "Did ya hear Del got into it with a copper last night? Caught 'im tryin' ta nick some veggies er somethin'. Threw 'im in the clinker."

"That what happened ta Del?" another man asked. "I always knew the law would catch up with 'im sooner or later. He's too bold, ya know that?"

"He coulda at least gone fer a pot roast t' make it worth his while 'stead of a couple ears o' corn."

A few guffaws ensued from the group.

"What is this world comin' to?" demanded Dorothy. "Del's just a boy, an' shame on all of you fer yer cold hearts. Ya just finish up a-praisin' the good Lord an' then act like wild dogs." She got up and hurried away in disgust.

Dorothy had unofficially adopted Del Hancock and had given him the love that she could no longer give to her deceased children or to the husband who had deserted her.

"Must be hard for 'er," Benjamin observed.

"Ya sure do hear 'bout a lotta sorrowful things seems like," Ronald muttered. "I saw just last Tuesday...or was it Wednesday? I ferget. Father kickin' his own son out o' the house. Heard 'im say, 'I can't afford it anymore, son. Ya gotta make yer own way now.' That man looked as heartbroken as 'is son did. Boy was only 'bout twelve, maybe thirteen. Felt awful sorry for the lad, I did. It just don't seem right, does it? This depression sure 'as a way o' makin' monsters outa men, I say." Ronald paused thoughtfully and added, "But I s'pose desperate times call fer desperate measures."

Most of Ronald's audience agreed.

"It ain't just the men what's causin' all the trouble. The kids is just as bad," Tom said. "'dja hear 'bout that chap on the corner o' Elm Street? Stole from 'is own Ma, he did. He'd o' had no end to 'is misery if'n 'is pa was still alive to give 'im a whoopin' for it, too. Stole his Ma's life savings and then up an' ran off."

"Yeah? Well, you do yer fair share o' stealin', too, Tom ol' boy," Ronald retorted.

"I don't steal from my Ma."

"We jaw about the Hancock boy and the fella who kicked 'is son out like we was better than them. Well, I've lived 'ere long enough t' know that ain't true," Ginny pointed out.

Dorothy returned hastily, clutching in her hands a few sheets of paper. Her demeanor had completely changed.

"Take a look at what some man gave me t' hand out 'round here," she said. "They're fliers for a soup kitchen. Free food on Mondays, Wednesdays, and Fridays!"

The fliers were passed around, and the excitement grew.

"Who's doing this soup kitchen?" asked Louise. "Who has enough money for it?"

"It's the banker's family. See, down here," Dorothy said, pointing a scrawny finger at the flier. "It says it's in the bank's basement."

"Oh, it's those conceited Maxwells," Joseph said distastefully. "I might've known they'd try somethin' like that. I knew the Maxwells when I still lived in town. I don't suppose a humble word ever came out of either one o' their mouths. Always trying to impress everyone."

"Tell me more about the Maxwells," Louise pressed.

"What's there to tell? They're just rich, conceited blowhards is what they are," grumbled Joseph. "I feel bad for their youngsters having to put up with it all."

"They have children, then?" asked Louise, growing more interested.

"Two. Don't recall their names, and it's been a long while since I've seen 'em. Must be around school-age now."

Sam, who had been sitting silently among the group, suddenly rose and tramped out of the camp without a word.

He's a roguish one, he is, Louise determined as she watched him go.

As conversation drifted to another topic, Louise thought to herself, *Yes, I do believe I shall pay a visit to this soup kitchen tomorrow.*

Chapter Sixteen:
Stormy Weather

At 6:00 in the morning, Rebecca was out of bed and in the kitchen reading her Bible and praying. "I need your guidance, Lord," she whispered. "Honestly, I'm just not sure how to manage Rhoda."

As Rebecca sat quietly for a few minutes, an idea slowly began to form in her mind. *Rhoda needs to feel valued and loved. How can I do that, Father? Hmm...something small at first, just to show her that she can be useful.*

Rebecca glanced around the kitchen, hoping to get an idea. Her eyes focused on Elijah's torn britches that sat on the counter waiting for repair. He had accidentally ripped a hole in them while playing with Dick and Andrew on Saturday, and Rebecca hadn't gotten around to fixing them yet. She considered teaching Rhoda how to mend clothes but decided against it since Rhoda might stick herself with the needle.

Rebecca's mind returned to the Maxwells when, suddenly, an idea popped into her head. *Of course! I'll teach Rhoda how to knit scarves for the soup kitchen!*

Rebecca was so pleased with her idea that she leaned back in the kitchen chair smugly until she remembered the idea had come to her in prayer. She hastily leaned forward, bowed her head, and added, *Thank You, Lord!*

Rebecca immediately got busy gathering yarn and knitting needles from her sewing basket. She was just setting the materials on the kitchen counter next to Elijah's pants when Elijah, himself, clad in his pajamas, stumbled into the kitchen, followed by James.

"Ith breakfatht ready?" Elijah asked drowsily.

At the same time, James announced, "I'm going out for a walk around the block, darling. I'll be back for breakfast." He kissed Rebecca's cheek.

"Breakfast should be ready in about twenty minutes. I'm making flapjacks today."

"Sounds good to me," said James as he laced his oxfords.

Rebecca whipped up some pancake batter. She enjoyed cooking, but a five-year-old boy bouncing around the kitchen at 6:30 a.m. set progress at a snail's pace.

After the second spill, Rebecca, in an attempt to drive the bundle of energy out of the kitchen, suggested, "Elijah, please make sure your sisters are getting up. Ruth and Anna have school today."

As the first steaming cake was flipped onto a plate, Elijah's footsteps were heard thundering down the stairs.

"Mitheth Olthon!" he exclaimed just as a loud crash echoed through the kitchen. Upon running in, he had accidentally tipped over a small, hand-painted vase containing the bouquet Ruth had picked for Rebecca on Saturday.

"What is it?" asked Rebecca, trying to hide her irritation and wishing it had taken Elijah more time to see if the girls were up. "Please don't run or shout like that in the house. Come here and help me pick up the pieces."

"Mitheth Olthon, ya gotta come. Ruth's cryin' and Rhoda's tantrumin'. Ya gotta come right away," Elijah explained, tugging on Rebecca's sleeve.

Rebecca, Rebecca, what have you gotten yourself into? Removing the pan from the stove, she hastily followed Elijah—and the sound of the ruckus—up to the attic.

"Rhoda Pauline Clayton! Stop it right now!" Anna's voice fired angrily.

You must be firm.

Jerking open the door, she was appalled at what she saw. Anna had her arms around Rhoda's waist, attempting to yank her away from Ruth. Ruth was screaming for help and crying. Rhoda was yelling and pulling Ruth's bouncy black curls.

"WHAT IS GOING ON?" Rebecca demanded fiercely. The strength of her voice stopped all action at once.

Everyone spoke at the same time.

"Rhoda pulled my hair," sobbed Ruth.

"It started when Ruth said—" Anna began, but Rhoda interrupted.

"It ain't my fault! Ruth started it. She hit me on my arm. On purpose!"

"That's not true!" Ruth cut in angrily. "I didn't mean ta hit her arm. I was getting dressed and I didn't know she was there, and she couldn't see me. I'm sorry, Mrs. Olson. Really. I didn't mean ta hurt Rhoda."

Rebecca was beside herself. Before she knew it, a Bible verse was spilling from her lips: "Proverbs 15:1: 'A soft answer turneth away wrath: but grievous words stir up anger.' I am going to continue making breakfast. I expect you all to put those words into practice. You are to find five nice things to say to one another. You are to forgive each other. And then you are to come downstairs to eat. Am I clear?"

"Yes, ma'am," Anna responded. "We're all very sorry."

Rebecca and Elijah returned to the kitchen.

"Can I help? Pleathe?" begged Elijah.

"Alright," agreed Rebecca, her heart desperately praying for both the situation with the girls and for breakfast-making with Elijah. *Did I just tell him 'all right'?*

"You may help me pour the batter into the pan. Be careful not to touch it. It's hot."

Boosting him up onto a chair, Rebecca showed him how to scoop out the batter and pour it into the pan. The sweet smell of breakfast cakes filled the kitchen. After a few more flapjacks had been made, James strolled in.

"Look, Pathtor Olthon! I made thothe flapjackth!" Elijah bragged, pointing to a clump of mutant cakes.

"Well, now. I'll be sure to have one that you made, then." James whistled a song as he removed his shoes.

"Can ya teach me how ta whithle?" implored Elijah.

63

"I can try, but it takes some practice. Put your lips like this and blow." Pastor Olson demonstrated.

Elijah tried, but to no avail.

"Lemme try it again."

While Pastor Olson distracted Elijah, Rebecca finished making the hotcakes. She had just flipped the last one onto the plate when all three girls marched down the stairs, neatly dressed, with solemn expressions on their faces. Rebecca greeted them as though nothing had happened. Anna and Ruth exchanged wide-eyed glances.

"Is all well, girls?"

"Y…yes, ma'am," Anna stammered, glancing sideways toward Pastor Olson.

James looked at the girls and then at his wife. "Is something wrong?"

"No," Rebecca said quickly. "We just had a little Bible lesson this morning on forgiveness."

"Ah," said Pastor Olson. "I see. Well, we'd better eat breakfast. Anna and Ruth need to get to school, and I'd better get to church."

As soon as breakfast was finished, Pastor Olson bid goodbye to all and strolled down the street toward the church. Rebecca handed Anna and Ruth their dinner pails and book bags. They were both giddy about their first day at a new school. Rebecca and Elijah waved to the girls as they hurried down the street in the direction of the tiny schoolhouse.

Just then, an all-too-familiar black car drove into the Olsons' driveway.

"Hello, Rebecca," Lucille Maxwell sang. "I bought some church clothes for those children, just as I said I would. I hope they fit alright. I had to guess at the sizes, you know."

"That really wasn't necessary."

"No. I said I would do it, and here they are. This dress is for the oldest girl, this for the youngest, and this for the blind one. And here's a proper suit for that boy."

"Thank you, Lucille. Elijah, what do you say?"

"I didn't thay nothin'."

"What should you say?"

"Hot diggity dog!"

Rebecca whispered something into Elijah's ear.

"Oh. Thank you, Mitheth Maxwell."

"Anytime. Now, I insist on taking Elijah to play with my Dick and Andrew this morning. I'll take all three to the soup kitchen at noon, and you may pick him up there."

Rebecca smiled wryly. "What would you like me to bring?"

"Bring?" sputtered Lucille.

"Yes. What shall I bring to the soup kitchen?"

"Why, I never said you had to volunteer to serve at the soup kitchen today. I just said that I'd bring Elijah with me and take the boys to the soup kitchen where you may pick him up. I wouldn't dream of tugging on people's consciences when they'd rather not volunteer."

Rebecca didn't respond, but she wore amusement on her face.

"Come, Elijah," Lucille said awkwardly, avoiding Rebecca's knowing look.

Now for Rhoda, Rebecca thought as Lucille's car disappeared from view.

Chapter Seventeen:
Useful Rhoda

Rebecca found Rhoda hunched in a corner in the living room, her head lowered, and her hands folded in her lap.

"Rhoda, come here, please," she directed.

Rhoda uncertainly followed Mrs. Olson's footsteps into the kitchen, not sure what to expect. Rebecca reached out and brushed a wisp of the girl's short brown hair out of her face, tucking it behind her ear. Rhoda's softened expression demonstrated that the child had calmed down dramatically from earlier that morning.

"I know it's difficult for you, dear."

"I wanna go to school, too. It's not fair that Ruth an' Anna can go an' learn things that I can't. Ruth is my little sister, an' she's gonna be smarter than me."

"That doesn't seem fair, does it. I've never been blind, so I can't imagine all that you're feeling. All I know is that you can't give up. When life gives us lemons, we need to do our best to make lemonade."

"We're makin' lemonade?" Rhoda asked, wrinkling up her nose in confusion.

"No, not exactly. Come out to the garden with me."

Rebecca took Rhoda's hand and led her down one of the stone paths that wove through the garden. Suddenly, Rebecca let go. Rhoda stopped, frozen in her tracks. Rebecca boldly strode a few yards ahead, turned around to face Rhoda, and called, "Come over here, and sit down on the bench with me."

Panic overtook Rhoda. She opened her mouth to protest.

"Take off your shoes and feel the cobblestones with your toes. Follow the path and come to me. I'm right here. I can see you. I know you can do it. Just try."

Although annoyed, Rhoda did as she was told. She removed her shoes and felt the cool, smooth stones under her feet. Cautiously, she began to walk in the direction of Rebecca's voice. When her feet touched vegetation, she cried out in alarm.

"I'm right here," Rebecca assured her calmly. "Just find the path again and keep going. You're almost here."

Rhoda continued on until she reached the bench and sat down.

Rebecca patted the girl's knee in congratulations and put a ball of something soft into her hands. "Can you guess what it is?" Rhoda could almost hear her smiling.

"It's yarn."

"That's right. And here's something else."

Rhoda grasped two long, wooden sticks with pointy ends.

"Knitting needles," Mrs. Olson explained. "I'm going to teach you how to knit, and you can work on making some warm hats and scarves for the needy people who come to the soup kitchen."

"But I can't—"

"I believe you can. I have knitted for so many years that I don't even have to look at my needles anymore. I will teach you how to feel the stitches like I do. You can do it, and you'll bless many people with your skill."

Well, I guess it's something to do, Rhoda reasoned.

The next half hour was spent making stitches and pulling them out until two long rows had been constructed.

Rhoda glowed as Rebecca praised her. She felt the ridges of the fabric that was coming together in her hands. Then, a cloud seemed to cross her face, and she threw the knitting down next to her.

"I can't do it. It's way too hard. I don't wanna learn to knit."

"That's up to you, but I would encourage you not to give up on it. It'll take some time getting used to it, but just think of how proud you will be when you can hold up that scarf and say, 'I made this!' Put it aside for now, and let's pick some flowers for the soup kitchen tables."

"Ain't you gonna put 'em in the contest?"

"No. I've entered these flowers in that contest for many years, and now I can see that there are much better uses for them. Get down on your hands and knees with me and feel for the flowers."

Rhoda obeyed. Rebecca took Rhoda's hand and smoothed her fingers over a blossom. Rhoda felt her way down the stem and snapped it off when her fingers had almost reached the ground. It was the first flower she'd picked since she had gone blind. Rhoda drew the flower to her nose and breathed in its rich perfume. She felt a motivation within her that she had not experienced for a long time. On her own, she figured out a method using touch, smell, and her knowledge of flowers to construct gorgeous bouquets in her hands as she visualized them in her mind. Together, Rhoda and Rebecca picked enough bouquets for five tables.

"Now, then," Rebecca said matter-of-factly. "I'll meet you in the house. Stand up, and I'll turn you in the right direction."

After making sure Rhoda was facing the entrance to the house, Rebecca hurried to the door and watched from just inside. At first, Rhoda did not move. Then, she slowly began to shuffle. Whenever her foot slipped off the path, she said nothing; instead, she righted herself and continued on.

Mrs. Olson doesn't treat me the same way everyone else does, Rhoda thought as she groped along. *She treats me like I'm just a normal girl. She challenges me.*

Strangely, Rhoda began to like it.

Chapter Eighteen:
The Soup Kitchen

Rhoda gripped a basket of flowers in one hand and clung to Rebecca's hand with the other. She had to walk swiftly to keep up with Mrs. Olson's healthy stride.

"We're almost there. Why, that's Elijah coming out of the bank!"

As Elijah ran up to them, he pointed back at a cardboard sign posted on the building. "What duth that thay?"

"It says 'Free Food for the Unemployed.' What are you doing out here by yourself? Where's Mrs. Maxwell?"

"I dunno. Thomewhere in the bathement. Come an' thee all the people!" he exclaimed.

The three walked down the steps of Maxwell Bank to the basement.

"Wait here with your brother. I'll be right back."

The echo of Mrs. Olson's sturdy shoes pounding against the concrete floor soon died away. Rhoda could almost taste the hot chicken soup and fresh, homemade bread. The room was warm and stuffy, and all of the commotion made her head swim. Suddenly, there was heavy breathing right next to Rhoda, followed by someone crashing into her. Rhoda cried out as she tumbled to the floor.

"Watch where yer going!" crackled a woman's raspy voice. "Kids these days, running around half-crazed and bumping into the elderly. What are two kids like you doing in this place anyway? Don't you know this is a soup kitchen? You git on home."

With Elijah's help, Rhoda managed to stand up.

"My thithter didn't bump into you. She wath jutht thtanding—"

"Don't be impertinent, young man."

"I'm sorry, ma'am. It won't happen again." Rhoda could hear her voice shaking with fright.

A man's voice from the food line called out, "Hey, Louise, it even looks edible!"

The woman grunted, mumbled something under her breath, and hurried toward the voice.

Rhoda was relieved to hear Mrs. Olson's footsteps returning.

"Who wath that lady?" asked Elijah fearfully.

"She's a homeless woman, Elijah. She certainly didn't seem very friendly, did she. Maybe she's just not used to children."

"She knocked my thithter down."

"Are you okay? Are you hurt?"

"I'm fine."

"Elijah, would you please help me put these flowers on the tables? We won't be staying because they already have enough volunteers today. We'll come back some other time. Rhoda, please wait here a moment. We'll be right back."

As Rhoda leaned against the wall, she overhead the voice of the woman who had knocked her down.

"Would you mind pointin' out the banker's family to me? I'd be very obliged if you would introduce me to those kindhearted folks," she was saying to a volunteer.

"Of course. Mrs. Maxwell and her boys are in the kitchen right now. Let me go and get them for you."

Rhoda heard Lucille's shrill voice and the scuttling feet of Dick and Andrew.

"Hello, there. What may I do for you?" Lucille asked in a sugary voice, loudly enough to ensure that others would notice her tenderness.

"I'd really like to thank you and your family for all of the hard work you put into all this. Providing food for unwanted souls like us is a great act of mercy." Louise made sure she was heard, as well.

"The credit really doesn't belong to us," Lucille replied, her voice increasing slightly in volume. Rhoda hated how

70

Lucille's words were the exact opposite of her thoughts. "The credit belongs to all of these volunteers," she continued with a sweep of her arm in a grand gesture. "Why, we're just humble servants doing our best to help those in need." Lucille concluded her speech with her hand over her heart.

"'course the credit belongs to you! You're the ones who offered up the basement of your bank for such a worthy cause."

"Yes, I suppose you're right about that. And of course, if we had never donated a large sum of money to get it started, I suppose it wouldn't have happened. Not that the cost was too high for a banker and his wife," Lucille added with airs.

"Your family really is a blessing to all of us," the crackly woman crooned. "Your children are precious. I always have loved children. I used to sing with my grandchildren. Well, that is, before poverty took them too soon." The woman's voice choked up.

Rhoda shook her head, trying to determine which of the two ladies was the better actress.

"I'm so sorry to hear that. Why don't you sing with Dick and Andrew. I'm sure they'd love that, wouldn't you, boys."

Dick stuck out his tongue at his mother, while Andrew stomped his foot crossly.

"That means so much to me. What a kind lady you are, and what sweet children you have."

Rhoda was disgusted.

♦   ♦   ♦

During supper, Anna and Ruth chatted ardently about their day at school.

"Miss Thomas is real nice," Ruth declared. "She plays with the kids at recess."

"Most of the kids are nice, too. Some of the older boys play tricks on the girls, but no one makes fun of anyone if they're not rich," put in Anna.

71

"There's twelve kids in our school. Seven of 'em are girls an' five of 'em are boys," Ruth announced. "There's a girl my age who told me that there used ta be more kids, but they had ta drop out ta help their families by gettin' jobs sellin' newspapers an' things. Ain't that sad?"

Rhoda was secretly relieved to hear that she wasn't the only one who couldn't go to school. *But those kids aren't blind.*

"I played with Dick an' Andrew today. They thure have lotth of toyth. They have a toy boat that can go in the water! We put it in the bird bath in their back yard, and it floated real good. But then Mitheth Maxwell thaid that we were gonna thcare the birdth away, tho we went inthide ta play with their toy airplane. Then we played with other toyth—they thure have got lotth of 'em! Then we went outthide an' we played war. Did you know that Dick an' Andrew never played war before? We got kinda dirty, though, an' I didn't think that Mitheth Maxwell would like that much, 'cauthe she didn't like it when we got dirty at your houth, Pathtor Olthon. We washed ourthelves off in the bird bath and climbed treeth inthtead 'til we dried off. Then we went ta the thoup kitchen, an' then Mitheth Olthon came and got me."

"Sounds like you had a good time," commented Pastor Olson. He could only imagine Lucille's reactions to the boys' fun and games.

Everyone was silent as they waited for Rhoda to tell about her day.

When she didn't say anything, Mrs. Olson informed them, "Rhoda had a busy day today. She learned how to walk in the garden by herself. She picked all kinds of flowers for the soup kitchen, and then we walked there to deliver them. Oh, and she made lemonade." Mrs. Olson patted Rhoda's hand to acknowledge their secret. "Rhoda, tell them what else you learned to do."

"Learned to knit," Rhoda mumbled. She waited to see what her siblings would say.

"You what? Really? You did? Lemme see!" Ruth exclaimed, every trace of the morning's hard feelings completely gone.

"I'm sure she'll show you the scarf she's making right after we finish eating."

"You can make all kinds of useful things," Anna gushed. "Mittens and hats and scarves. Won't Mother be proud of you?"

Rhoda didn't respond, but she brightened a little as she continued eating.

Chapter Nineteen:
A Letter From Mother

Ka-BOOM!

Thunder awoke everyone the next morning. Unfortunately, it didn't take long for Rhoda's mood to match the weather.

Rhoda sat in her attic room near the window listening to the rain pattering on the glass panes. Through the cloudburst, she heard the faint rumble of the Olsons' car pulling out of the driveway. Pastor Olson was driving Anna and Ruth to school due to the weather. As Mrs. Olson and Elijah called their goodbyes from downstairs, Rhoda's mind shouted miserably, *Why can't I go to school?! Why can't I do the things Anna and Ruth can?!*

Mrs. Olson's footsteps sounded at the bottom of the stairs.

"Rhoda, come downstairs with Elijah and me. I'm sure we can find something fun for us all to do."

"Like what?" Rhoda asked with a sniffle.

"Why don't you find your knitting. That's something fun to do on a rainy day."

"I told you. Knitting's too hard. I don't wanna do it anymore," Rhoda replied defiantly.

"Suit yourself," Mrs. Olson stated as she returned to join Elijah.

Rhoda was angry. She had expected Mrs. Olson to feel sorry for her and try to comfort her the way everyone else did. Rhoda was used to being bathed with sympathy from her mother, her aunt, and the people she knew back at home. Everyone felt sorry for her.

They care about me, Rhoda grumbled inwardly. *Mrs. Olson doesn't. She doesn't even care that I'm blind.*

Rhoda stomped haltingly over to her dresser and pulled her wooden trinket box out of the drawer. She had found that it soothed her to trace the lilies with her fingers. Absentmindedly, Rhoda reached back into the drawer. When she brushed against the soft, partially knit scarf, her own heart rebuked her.

Who took the time to teach me to knit? Who challenges me to do things that normal children can do? Tears choked her. *Who believes that, even though I'm blind, I can be just as useful as anyone else?*

The shame Rhoda felt compelled her down the stairs and steered her toward the kitchen. She hesitated at the doorway and listened to Mrs. Olson's melodious voice humming what sounded like a hymn from church.

Steeling herself, Rhoda ambled into the room and cleared her throat. Mrs. Olson's humming stopped, and Rhoda knew she was looking at her.

"I'm...I'm...I..." She blushed deeply.

Mrs. Olson came to the rescue. "I see you brought your knitting. Come sit by me and I'll teach you how to purl. Purling is just the opposite of knitting."

The hours flew by as Rhoda worked stitch after stitch until it was almost time for Ruth and Anna to come home. The rain had stopped, and the birds had begun to chirp. Rhoda listened to their jovial songs as she sat on the front porch with her half-knitted scarf. An earthy post-rain scent floated on the cool breeze. Elijah was in the back yard searching in the wet soil for worms, and Mrs. Olson was sweeping the front walk free of the debris that had blown in with the storm.

"I see a few branches in the yard. Rhoda, let's play a game. I'll stand right here on the porch, and you follow my directions to find and pick up the sticks. It should be fun, and it'll also be helpful to me to have the sticks picked up."

Rhoda found herself agreeing, much to her own surprise.

Mrs. Olson directed her: "Go right. Now take a left turn. Just keep going straight."

Rhoda picked up the sticks all by herself.

Before long, exclamations of delight could be heard as Anna and Ruth trotted up to the porch.

"Hello, girls! How was school today?" Mrs. Olson asked them.

"It was swell! For homework, I get ta read a story from my McGuffey Reader," Ruth told her.

"I have to study geography and Latin. I wish I could read the McGuffey stories instead," Anna smirked. "But school was the bee's knees," she added quickly.

Elijah sauntered around the corner of the house with a handful of worms.

Anna eyed his discoveries. "Ick! Leave those things on the ground where they belong."

"Thay, d'ya wanna hold one of my wormth, Mitheth Olthon?"

"Sure, I will," she replied, picking a plump one out of Elijah's hand.

"Do you really like those things?" Ruth asked in amazement.

"No, I wouldn't say I like them. But I'm used to them because I have four brothers. You can about imagine that, being the only girl, I'd be used to things such as worms and bugs," Mrs. Olson replied. "Here you go, Elijah. Now why don't you take them back where you found them."

"Can I jutht keep Harold for a pet?" Elijah begged. "I promithe I'll feed 'im and take care of 'im."

"No, I think you'd better put them all back. They'll be happier outside where they can have all kinds of room to tunnel around in the dirt. Do you think they'd be happy living in a jar?"

"No, I thuppothe they wouldn't," Elijah replied glumly. "I'll go an' put 'em back."

"That's a good boy. Now, since you can't keep your worms, how would you like to help Pastor Olson catch some fireflies tonight? You may put them in a jar and watch them glow for a while before you set them free."

"Hot diggity dog!" shouted Elijah, galloping to the back yard.

Rhoda held up her pile of sticks. "Where should I put 'em?"

"I'll take those. Why don't you tell the girls about the game we played."

Rhoda described the game.

"Can we put the sticks back out in the yard an' play, too? We could wear scarves for blindfolds. Please?" begged Ruth.

"That sounds like a fun idea. Yes, you may."

As the children had races in the wet grass to see who could follow the directions best, Pastor Olson's car rolled up the street.

"What're you playing?" he asked, slamming the car door shut.

"Play it with uth!" Elijah pleaded after explaining the rules.

"That sounds like the cat's meow! Count me in."

The children roared with laughter as a blindfolded Pastor Olson stumbled around trying to find the sticks. Even Rhoda broke out laughing when he declared that he was lost in his own front yard.

Mrs. Olson came back outside to watch her husband's antics. "Not very good at following directions, dear?" she teased.

"I guess not. Imagine how lost I would be if no one gave me directions." Pastor Olson removed his blindfold and re-oriented himself to face the group. "Kind of like the Bible in a way, isn't it? Without the Bible we'd be lost. We wouldn't really understand what's right and wrong, true and false, good and evil. We'd be spiritually blind."

"Nicely put," Rebecca agreed. "You all come inside now. Supper's on the table, and I don't want it to get cold."

As Rebecca cleared the table after the meal, Pastor Olson announced, "A letter arrived today from your mother. Shall I read it to you?"

"Yes, please!" beseeched Ruth.

Extracting his reading glasses from his pocket and placing them on his nose, Pastor Olson read the letter.

Dear Anna, Rhoda, Ruth, and Elijah,

This letter will have to be short because I have just arrived in Lakeview. I have secured a ride to Aunt Bette's house from one of her neighbors who happened to be in town.

I just wanted you to know that I got here safely, and I'll soon see Charity. Please be good for the Olsons, and remember your manners.

Sending much love,
Mother

A hush fell as the children drank in the words.

"I hope she writes again ta let us know how Charity's doin'," Ruth said wistfully.

"I'm sure she will," Mrs. Olson assured the children.

Chapter Twenty:
Volunteers

Wednesday afternoon found Rebecca, Elijah, and Rhoda volunteering at the Maxwell soup kitchen. Mrs. Olson put on her apron and immediately began slicing a loaf of homemade bread. This time, the hustle and bustle didn't bother Rhoda as much. She sat quietly in a corner working on her scarf and enjoying the spicy aroma of the chili. Occasionally, she made a mistake and Mrs. Olson had to pull out a row of knitting for her, but Rhoda didn't mind as long as she had something to do.

Wandering around the kitchen, Elijah was more of an impediment than a help. After a few incidents, Mrs. Maxwell sent Elijah out to sweep the walk by the front doors of the bank. After unintentionally smacking the window with the long broom handle, Elijah was grudgingly accepted back inside. Mrs. Olson couldn't help but marvel over how one sweet little boy could wreak so much havoc.

As the crowd filtered in, Rhoda's skin began to crawl. She had detected the voice of the woman who had knocked her over on Monday.

"Let's sing a song together, boys," she coaxed Dick and Andrew.

"We're helpin'," replied Andrew, fumbling for an excuse.

"You're such gentlemen to help your nice mother out. You deserve to take a break," the woman persisted.

Rhoda frowned. *Who would want to sing with that woman, anyway?*

"We don't wanna sing with you," whined Dick, who apparently agreed with Rhoda.

Just then, Rhoda heard someone sweep in and announce, "I'm from the *Briggsville Daily Register*, and I'd like to run a story on the soup kitchen. Is Mrs. Lucille Maxwell here at the moment?"

"Welcome!" called Lucille, hurrying out of the kitchen, smoothing down her apron and fluffing the mink trim on her dress all at the same time.

The man grunted. Rhoda heard him flip open a notepad. Sitting only a few feet away, she could hear every word of the interview.

"This soup kitchen has done wonders for those of us who are less fortunate," a crackly voice broke in, "and we've got Mrs. Maxwell here to thank for it all. I've never met a more caring lady with such dear little children as Mrs. Maxwell. Thank you on behalf of all of us."

"Now, really, let's be sensible," Mrs. Maxwell reasoned. "All I did was pay the sum of money to get it started. And, of course, it wouldn't have been possible without the use of my husband's bank."

As Lucille continued to chatter to the reporter, Rhoda heard the crackly-voiced woman join the out-of-work people waiting for bowls of chili.

A man in line sarcastically murmured, "Nice line, Louise. You tryin' to butter up that Maxwell woman? Maybe ya want her to do something for ya, eh? Well, good luck to ya. Them Maxwells got more pride in 'em than a peacock. You can stroke their pride, ya can, but ya can't get their money 'less there's somethin' in it fer them."

"Hey, we all gotta play our own angles, Joseph," hissed Louise.

Rhoda set her knitting in her lap and strained to hear more. What was this woman trying to do? Chills danced down her spine.

Chapter Twenty-One:
At Bette's House

Bette gingerly brushed her hand along Charity's fiery red cheek. Charity squirmed, her eyes sealed tightly. Chills shook her body as the fever blazed. She moaned and grumbled something before being hurled back into a feverish sleep.

Pauline hunched over the table nearby, scrawling a letter to her children. Her *American Pocket Medical Dictionary* sat open nearby.

"I wish Arthur was here. He'd be devastated if something were to happen and..." Bette hid her face in her hands and didn't complete her sentence.

"The only thing we can do is pray that the Lord will spare her," Pauline replied softly as she rose and placed a hand on her sister's shoulder. "It's about time we get some fresh water on that cloth for her forehead."

Bette was numb.

After doing what she could to make Charity more comfortable, Pauline turned her attention back to the letter. She read to herself what she had written, wishing that she had good news to share.

Dear Anna, Rhoda, Ruth, and Elijah,

I trust everything is going well at the Olsons' house.

There isn't much news, as Charity remains very ill.

Are Anna and Ruth enjoying school,

and are Rhoda and Elijah finding plenty
of nice things to do to keep them busy?

I'll see you just as soon as Charity gets
better.

I'm sure you're all having a grand time.

Lovingly,
Mother

Looking up from her letter, Pauline assured her sister, "Charity's a strong girl." Her voice sounded anything but confident.

Chapter Twenty-Two:
The Petersons

Nothing much happened during the rest of the week. Anna and Ruth went to school. Pastor Olson went to work. Rhoda, Elijah, and Mrs. Olson stayed at home. After supper, they'd do whatever they could dream up to amuse themselves before evening Bible reading and prayer.

Sunday had rolled around again, and the house was abuzz with excitement. The Petersons would be arriving in the afternoon. The children dressed for church in the new clothes Mrs. Maxwell had bought for them.

Ruth swished the skirt of her frock and touched the satin bow in her hair. "Ain't it beautiful, Anna? We've never been so dolled-up in our lives!"

"And how! I didn't know they made such pretty things," Anna agreed, adjusting the pleats in her blue dress.

"And mine's even pink! My favorite color!"

"Yes, they're very nice clothes. It was nice of Mrs. Maxwell to get them for you," Mrs. Olson said, only half listening. She was busy trying to wipe an oatmeal stain off of Elijah's new Sunday suit.

"I feel all funny in thith thing," Elijah remarked as Mrs. Olson continued to scrub.

"You'll get used to it after a while."

"But what if I can't get out? It'th awful tight."

"You'll get out of it. Here. Let me fix your collar and you'll feel better."

"Can I go outthide, pleathe?" asked Elijah, squirming around and scratching where the collar tickled his neck.

"Not now. We'll be going to church in a minute," Mrs. Olson replied. "I think that's the best we can do. There's still a smudge, but it'll have to do until wash day."

Rhoda was anything but pleased with her dress. She didn't see the point of wearing it if she couldn't even see it. The stiff fabric irritated her shoulders, and the bow yanked her hair so much that she wished she could rip it out. *I'd much rather be comfortable.*

"I don't wanna wear this thing," she murmured under her breath to Anna.

"You have to. Mrs. Maxwell bought it for you, and you have to wear it to church to show her that you're glad that she got it for you."

"But I'm not glad that she got it for me."

"Well, pretend you are, and stop complaining."

"Ready to go?" Pastor Olson strolled into the living room, buttoning his cuffs. He grinned when he saw Elijah's suit. "Were you trying to save some of that tasty oatmeal for later?"

"No. I didn't mean ta thpill it, but I geth it jutht jumped offa my thpoon," Elijah replied in a serious voice.

All the way to church, Anna and Ruth, delighted with their new clothes, sat up straight and tall in the back seat of the Olsons' Ford. Rhoda and Elijah mostly fidgeted. Pastor and Mrs. Olson exchanged amused glances in the front seat.

♦　　♦　　♦

Between Elijah and Ruth, Rhoda slumped and scowled. *Church is the most boring thing ever!* she wanted to shout. She was tired of sitting and listening to Pastor Olson's long sermon. Furthermore, she hated all the fussy little bows on her dress and feared they'd come off if she moved wrong. She had never liked to dress up and was almost glad that her family was poor so she didn't have to wear store-bought clothes every day. Rhoda held her handkerchief to her nose to block out the smell of a lady's overpowering lavender perfume until Ruth took the handkerchief away. The hot, sticky air in the building only added to her discomfort. She kicked her foot a little in frustration and sank back in the hard, wooden pew.

Anna whispered something to Ruth. Ruth leaned over and whispered, "Anna says to sit still."

"Dry up," Rhoda shot back crossly.

After what seemed to Rhoda an eternity and a half, Pastor Olson finally prayed a closing prayer. Immediately following the service, Mrs. Olson and the children strode briskly home to prepare for their company. Pastor Olson would fetch the Petersons in the car.

Anna, Ruth, and Mrs. Olson set to work preparing the meal and setting the table. Rhoda bided her time on the front porch, and Elijah wandered aimlessly.

"Ruth, you slice up the bread," Anna told her sister as she pulled a steaming pan of meatloaf out of the oven. "It's a little burnt, Mrs. Olson. Do you think it'll be okay?"

Rebecca put down her dishcloth and looked at the meatloaf. "It's fine," she assured Anna, dunking a spoon into the dishwater. "A little toasty around the edges, but it'll taste good."

"I've never made meatloaf before," said Anna as she covered the pan to keep in the heat. "I think I need a little more practice."

"You did a wonderful job. Everyone will love it."

"I hope so," Anna fretted.

Rhoda squirmed to get comfortable on the porch step. It was a difficult task while she was restrained by her church clothes. *I can't believe I have to wear this thing all day,* she griped to herself.

"Purdy, purdy," a cardinal sang.

"Thanks," grumbled Rhoda sarcastically.

"Thay, Rhoda," said Elijah as he came around to the front of the house. "Can you pleathe get my button back on? It fell off while I wath playin' in the dirt."

"You were playing in the dirt in your good Sunday suit?"

"Mitheth Olthon told me ta keep it on 'cauthe we're havin' comp'ny."

Rhoda sighed. "Go ask Mrs. Olson. I can't sew it on."

85

"Here they come!" Elijah hooted, tossing his button onto the porch. He jumped up and down and waved his arms.

Rhoda heard car doors click open and slam shut.

Elijah was suddenly still.

"What is it, Elijah?"

"Mithter Peterthon only hath one arm!"

"What?" asked Rhoda in disbelief.

"He duth! He jutht hath one arm, an' hith other thleeve ith all tied up!"

It can't be the Petersons, Rhoda told herself. *How can a man with only one arm carve so beautifully? And yet, who else could it be?*

Elijah ran up to meet them. "Mithter Peterthon, what happened ta your arm?" he shouted, pointing.

Mr. Peterson knelt down to Elijah's level. He furrowed up his face and looked confused. "I could've sworn I brought it with me. Eileen, have you seen my arm somewhere?" He peered under the car and in his shoe.

"No, dear. I haven't," Mrs. Peterson played along. "Maybe you left it at home."

Elijah's eyes grew round as saucers, and his jaw dropped open. "Really, Mithter Peterthon?"

The Petersons and Pastor Olson roared.

"No, son. I was just foolin' around a little," explained Mr. Peterson as soon as he had collected himself. "I'll tell you all about it after we eat."

"Will you, Mithter Peterthon?"

"Sure. Now I'd like to meet everyone and have a bite of that delicious meal you've fixed. Mmmm-mmm! I can almost taste it from here."

The cooks stood in the doorway, wiping their hands on their aprons.

"Thank you so much for the presents, Mr. and Mrs. Peterson," Anna raved. "Your carving is wonderful."

"Yes, thank you," Ruth jumped in. "I have my pressed flowers in my box. They almost match the carving."

"My train workth thwell. Pathtor Olthon helped me make trackth for it."

"Did he, now. I'll have to see those."

"Do you have something special in your box, Rhoda?" Mrs. Peterson asked kindly.

"Yes," Rhoda responded quietly. "I keep my shell necklace in it."

"I'll bet your necklace is very special to you," Mrs. Peterson replied.

"Uh-huh," Rhoda answered without explanation.

Mrs. Olson invited everyone into the kitchen and seated the group at the table. After complimenting the cooks, the adults conversed about the farmers' revolt and the upcoming election.

Before long, everyone gathered in the garden to hear Mr. Peterson's story.

"See, I lost this ol' arm of mine in the war. Did your pa ever tell you about the war?" he asked Elijah who hung on every word.

"No. He died when I wath a baby, but Mithter Brown told me 'bout the gunth an' thtuff when he went ta war. Didja really go ta war, Mithter Peterthon?"

"I did, and you wouldn't believe how many guns and fighter planes and warships and tanks there were. And miles upon miles o' muddy, rotten trenches. Barbed wire piled up everywhere. I'll tell ya, it got pretty rough at times."

"Didja get ta wear a uniform?" asked Elijah.

"Yes, sir. Still have it, too. It has shiny brass buttons."

"What happened ta yer arm?" Elijah asked impatiently.

"Well, now, I was just getting 'round to that, young man. 'Bout six months into the fray, we got tangled up in a pretty rough battle. Bullets were flying around us like a nest of hornets. This arm just got stung, I suppose."

"Did thomeone shoot it clear off?"

"No, not exactly. It got shot alright. There I was, bleeding on the ground. I thought it was the end of me, but one of my good friends risked his life to drag me out of the crossfire. He was shot dead. Never did get a chance to thank 'im."

Mr. Peterson had to pause a minute before continuing. "I was put in the field hospital, and my arm got infected. They had to cut it off, or I probably would've died."

"Did they cut it off with a thaw Mithter Peterthon?" asked Elijah.

Anna bristled. "Elijah! Remember your manners."

"But I wath jutht wondering," the boy replied meekly.

"Weren't ya scared when ya got shot?" asked Ruth.

"I was plenty scared. But lying there in the field hospital with only one arm seemed even worse at the time. I was feelin' awful sorry for myself. I says to myself, 'What good am I with just one arm? I'll never be useful. My life is over.'"

Rhoda breathlessly turned her entire attention to Mr. Peterson. She knew those feelings all too well. "What did you do?"

"Well, I couldn't exactly get my arm back, so I thought I'd make the best of things. God wasn't at all surprised that I lost my arm. He had a plan for me when I had two arms, and I knew He still had a plan for me with only one."

"But why does God let bad things like that happen? Why did God make Daddy die an' me go blind an' Charity get sick an' you lose your arm?" Rhoda's voice escalated with distress. "How can He love people like Pastor Olson says if He does such...such...mean things?" Rhoda accused in a final rush of emotion which surprised even herself.

"God doesn't enjoy watching us suffer," Mr. Peterson explained tenderly. "It isn't His fault. People suffer because people have chosen to disobey God. The Bible tells us that God originally made the world a perfect place. When the first two people—Adam and Eve—sinned, our perfect world was ruined. That's why there's pain and sickness and death in our world today. It's our own fault for rebelling against God who made us and loves us."

88

Eileen spoke. "James, maybe you could read the story in John chapter nine to us. That's the passage that first brought Wayne to the realization that we don't always understand why bad things happen, but God knows, and we can trust Him."

Rhoda, who normally didn't want anything to do with the Bible, found herself interested.

"Be right back," called Pastor Olson, already opening the screen door. A moment later, he returned with his Bible and settled in.

"'As Jesus passed by, he saw a man which was blind from his birth. And his disciples asked him, saying, Master, who did sin, this man, or his parents, that he was born blind? Jesus answered, Neither hath this man sinned, nor his parents: but that the works of God should be made manifest in him. I must work the works of him that sent me, while it is day: the night cometh, when no man can work. As long as I am in the world, I am the light of the world. When he had thus spoken, he spat on the ground, and made clay of the spittle, and he anointed the eyes of the blind man with the clay, and said unto him, Go, wash in the pool of Siloam, which is by interpretation, Sent. He went his way therefore, and washed, and came seeing. The neighbours therefore, and they which before had seen him that he was blind, said, Is not this he that sat and begged? Some said, This is he: others said, He is like him: but he said, I am he. Therefore said they unto him, How were thine eyes opened? He answered and said, A man that is called Jesus made clay, and anointed mine eyes, and said unto me, Go to the pool of Siloam, and wash: and I went and washed, and I received sight.'"

"Why was the man born blind?" quizzed Mrs. Peterson after Pastor Olson closed the leather cover of his Bible.

"So Jesus could heal 'im," offered Ruth perceptively.

"Then why didn't He jutht make the man have good eyeth if He wath gonna heal 'im anywayth?"

"This man had a very special purpose, Elijah," Mrs. Peterson explained. "Someone had to be born blind so Jesus could show everyone that He is God! One way He showed this was by healing a problem no one had ever been able to heal before. That man had a very important reason for being born blind, indeed. God has a purpose for all of us. We might think that something bad in our lives cannot possibly be useful, but often, God takes those bad things and uses them for much good."

Pastor Olson added, "Matthew 10:29-31 says, 'Are not two sparrows sold for a farthing? and one of them shall not fall on the ground without your Father. But the very hairs of your head are all numbered. Fear ye not therefore, ye are of more value than many sparrows.' Nothing happens to us without God knowing. He's always there with us, loving us and helping us, even when things are difficult or scary."

"You mean like when Mrs. Olson taught me to feel the garden path with my feet an' follow her voice? She was right there with me, makin' sure that I was safe."

"Exactly," Mrs. Peterson agreed, nodding her head.

Silence followed as the children seemed deep in thought.

"Ya wanna see the trackth Pathtor Olthon helped me make for my train?" asked Elijah, breaking the stillness.

"Absolutely," Mr. Peterson replied.

"Then will ya teach me how ta carve with my pocket knife?"

"One thing at a time, young man. Let's see about those train tracks, and then Mrs. Peterson and I should be getting home."

"Awwww…" Elijah and Ruth chorused in disappointment.

"I'll help do up those dishes," offered Mrs. Peterson, rising to her feet. "You made such a lovely meal, girls."

"We'll do the dishes later, Eileen. Please relax, and be our guest," Mrs. Olson responded.

"Nonsense. I'm glad to help."

Everyone went inside except Rhoda, who chose to stay by herself in the garden. One question repeated itself in her mind: *Could God possibly have made me blind for a purpose?*

Chapter Twenty-Three:
A Purpose?

That night, after Pastor Olson had returned from taking the Petersons home, Rhoda sat curled up on the couch with the box Mr. Peterson had made for her. The elaborate carvings told her that he had spent a lot of time on it. He had made it especially for her, and he had even carved her name on it. As Rhoda traced the *R*, a realization hit her for the first time. *I don't deserve something as beautiful as this. I'm always miserable and rude. Even though I'm blind, that's no excuse.*

Rhoda began to sob uncontrollably. She didn't care that everyone could see.

A pair of arms reached around and cradled her.

"Tell me what's wrong," Mrs. Olson urged. Her rhythmic side-to-side rocking calmed Rhoda as she slowly began to put into words the heavy weight that pressed on her.

"I'm sorry for how I treated you an' Pastor Olson an' my family. I wasn't really mad at you. I was mad at God fer makin' me blind. Do you really think God has a purpose for me like Mrs. Peterson said? That I'm not worthless an' forgotten?"

Pastor Olson's deep voice answered her. "Rhoda, you are not worthless and you are surely not forgotten. God loves you more than anyone else could ever love you."

"Even more than Mother?" Elijah questioned, wide-eyed.

"Yes. Even more."

"But, how do you know?" Rhoda demanded.

"Rhoda, do you remember how Mr. Peterson's friend died trying to save him?"

"Mmm-hmm."

"Mr. Peterson lost an arm, but he didn't lose his life. Mr. Peterson probably would have died out on that field. Instead, his friend died in his place so Mr. Peterson could live. Well, God did the same for you."

The children pressed in closer, eagerly listening.

"Jesus, who is God, came into this sin-cursed world to rescue you and me and all people. God loves you so much that He chose to die a horrible death for you...in your place. Just like Mr. Peterson's friend."

"But I ain't never been shotted at," Elijah observed, confused.

"No, you haven't. But there's something far worse than being shot at or losing an arm or going blind. God saved you from the worst thing ever."

"How?" asked Anna.

"Let me read you a very special book."

Pastor Olson strode into his study. A moment later, he came out holding a small, homemade book bound with yarn. He handed it to Elijah who opened it at once and flipped through the pages.

"But there's nothin' there," commented Ruth as she leaned over to take a look.

"Oh, but there is," Pastor Olson replied. "These colors each mean something."

Rhoda protested, "I can't even see the pages."

"Pastor Olson will tell you the colors. Come over and listen," Anna told her sister.

"This first page is a gold color. Gold reminds us of heaven."

"Why duth it remind uth of heaven?" Elijah questioned.

"It reminds us of heaven because in heaven, everything is bright and beautiful. Nobody is ever sad or angry in heaven. Heaven is a perfect place. Heaven is God's home. I know all of that because we can read about heaven in the Bible."

"I won't even be able to see heaven. I'm blind!"

"Rhoda, in heaven, everyone who is blind or deaf or sick will be healed. Just as Jesus healed the blind man in the story we read, He will one day heal all of us, inside and out."

"You mean I won't be blind forever?" Hope began to rise within her.

"What's the next page?" asked Ruth.

"The next page is a black color. The black reminds us of something called sin."

"What'th that?" asked Elijah.

"Sin is anything we do that God says is wrong. If you say or do something bad, that's sin. The saddest part about sin is that it keeps us out of heaven. Heaven is a beautiful place without any sin in it. Instead of going to heaven, people who sin have to go to a very bad place called the lake of fire. Romans 3:23 says, 'For the wages of sin is death.' We have to die because of our sin. We can't go to heaven."

"But we can go ta heaven if we're really good, right?" Ruth piped up.

"No, Ruth. Even if you're really good, you still can't go to heaven. Even if you only sin a little bit, you can't get in."

Rhoda's stomach turned. *I sin so much. I do all kinds of bad things. I won't go to heaven, and I'll always be blind.*

"Then no one could get to heaven, could they?" Ruth remarked forlornly. "Not even a pastor, right?"

"Not even a pastor. Because we all sin, we can't go to heaven. But there's good news. God loves us so much, that He decided to make a way for us to go to heaven."

Pastor Olson flipped the page in the book. "This page is red. Red reminds us of Jesus. Jesus left His wonderful heaven and came to sinful earth. Jesus never sinned at all because Jesus is God, and God is perfect. People on earth killed Jesus in a terrible way. But that was all part of God's plan. Jesus died in our place because that was the only way He could get rid of our sin problem. He died so we could be rescued."

"Just like the man who died to save Mr. Peterson's life?" Anna questioned.

"Just like that."

"That's so sad," Ruth lamented.

93

"It is, but something amazing happened. Jesus didn't stay dead! Because He is God, He came back to life three days later. This next page is white. John 3:16 says, 'For God so loved the world, that he gave his only begotten Son, that whosoever believeth in him should not perish, but have everlasting life.' If we trust God to forgive us from our sins—if we believe that Jesus died and came back to life in order to pay the price for our sins—then we can go to heaven. It's as simple as that. God promises to wash away our sins and make us even cleaner than this white paper."

"Ith my daddy in heaven?"

"Oh, yes, Elijah. I know that your daddy loved Jesus very much. He believed that Jesus died to take away his sins. And if you believe that, too, then you will see your daddy again someday in heaven."

"We will?!" Ruth jumped to her feet.

"Can we really see Daddy again?" asked Rhoda.

"Yes. If you really believe that Jesus died to take away your sins, you will go to heaven. You will see him there. And best of all, you'll be with Jesus forever."

"Hot diggity dog!" Elijah jumped up and down.

"When we trust Jesus, He promises to be right here with us, helping us to live in a good way until it's our time to go to heaven. He keeps us on a good path. Jesus is our Helper and Friend."

"He ith?"

"Yes. Jesus cares for you and loves you."

"Can I be Jethuth' friend, too? Duth He like turtleth an' wormth an' mud?"

"He made those turtles and worms and mud, Elijah. I'm sure He likes them as much as you do," Mrs. Olson replied, tussling the boy's hair.

"Pastor Olson," Rhoda began shyly. "Can I be Jesus' friend, too? Will He ever forgive me for being angry at Him?"

"Yes, He will. Jesus forgives us from all of our sins. He wipes away every sin we've ever done. And He knows about all the sins we'll do tomorrow. And the next day. And the

94

next. And He forgives those sins, too. No sin is so big that God can't forgive us from it."

"How do I ask God to forgive me?" Rhoda asked.

"Just ask Him. Tell Him that you believe that Jesus died for your sins and came back to life," Pastor Olson explained. "Want me to pray with you?"

As Pastor Olson prayed with the children, Rhoda's misery began to be replaced by a strange sort of peace and...dare she say...even joy! How good it felt to stand clean before the God who had not abandoned her after all. He had even sacrificed His own life to save her! She felt like she was beginning a brand new life.

♦ ♦ ♦

After the children had been tucked into bed, Rebecca lay awake. A thought struck her: *I've suffered for a purpose, too. God didn't allow me to have children because He knew a whole lot better than I did. If I would have had children, perhaps the Clayton children would never have come to live with us, and they might never have come to know the Savior. God used something that I thought was terrible and made it into something wonderful!*

Rebecca felt relief flood her heart as she suddenly found herself able to say the words that had for so long seemed impossible to utter.

Thank you, Lord, for making me barren!

Chapter Twenty-Four:
A Plan

The following days showed an amazing change in Rhoda. She thirsted to know more about this Jesus who had rescued her. Rhoda searched for anything she could do to help Mrs. Olson in order to have time to sit in the garden and read from the Bible together. On Wednesday morning, Mrs. Olson read the story of the Good Samaritan and told Rhoda and Elijah, who was also listening to the story, how important it is to serve others.

"Can you think of any ways we can serve others today?" Mrs. Olson asked.

Elijah jumped up. "Let'th go help at the thoup kitchen again!"

Rhoda agreed. "I can serve people by making hats an' scarves since I can't help with the food. At least not yet," she added determinedly.

By 10:30, Rebecca, Rhoda, and Elijah were again at the soup kitchen. Rebecca cooked, and Elijah ran around underfoot until someone came up with the idea of having him escort people to the food line. Rhoda sat knitting in a chair at the top of the stairs. Inspired by Mr. Peterson's carving ability, Rhoda worked to sharpen her knitting skills so that she very seldom needed Mrs. Olson's help anymore. Her fingers flew nimbly along, and soon, a new hat or scarf would take shape.

"Thith way, ma'am. They're therving real good thoup today," Rhoda heard her brother say. She smiled as she pictured chubby little Elijah ushering a lady to the food line.

Rhoda heard the door open again, and a puff of refreshing breeze washed over her.

"Uncle Arthur!" Elijah shouted, startling Rhoda so much that she dropped her knitting.

"Arthur, eh?" Rhoda recognized the woman's crackly voice immediately.

"Elijah? Elijah Clayton?" the man inquired hesitantly. "Elijah!" After scooping up the spunky five-year-old and swinging him around, Arthur noticed the girl knitting. "Rhoda!" He reached out to her. Not expecting the greeting, she flinched. "Rhoda?"

There was a cloudy look in her eyes.

"Yes," Rhoda replied, swallowing hard. "Uncle Arthur, I...I can't see you. I...I got brain fever, an'..." Her voice trailed off.

When Arthur realized Rhoda's situation, his happiness turned to distress. "What're you doing here? Where's your mother and Anna and Ruth?"

Before Rhoda could answer, Elijah blurted, "Ruth an' Anna are in thchool. Charity'th awful thick, an' Mother went ta help Aunt Bette. She thent uth here ta live with the pathtor until Charity ith better."

Rhoda nudged Elijah, but the truth was out.

"Charity's sick? What do you mean? How long?" Uncle Arthur frantically threw the questions at his niece and nephew.

The news hit Arthur like a freight train. Anguished, he exited the bank.

"You kids stay here, got it?" demanded Louise harshly as she followed Arthur. A plan was brewing in her mind.

"Sam, er, Arthur," she corrected herself, "pull yourself together. You've gotta get some quick dough for a doctor for your girl."

"Don't you think I know that?" Arthur retorted sharply.

"I know just how you can get that money."

"I suppose you have a gold nugget tucked in your shoe with that newspaper. Leave me alone."

"I can get you that money."

Arthur didn't respond.

Louise continued, "Lindbergh baby."

97

"What?" Arthur shot Louise a look as if she were half-crazed.

"Lindbergh baby."

"I don't know what you're talking about, and I would guess neither do you."

"You listen up. Them Maxwells got a full pocket and then some. Here's how we'll do it. This Friday, I'll lure the Maxwell boys out here into the alley. You grab 'em, and we'll tie 'em up so they don't get away. Look, I got it made so they won't even suspect us. It'll be a clean sweep. Duck soup!"

"You mean snatch the Maxwell boys? And get ransom money?" asked Arthur.

"Arthur, you're behind the eight ball. Ya wanna just stand by and let that girl of yours die, or are you gonna help me?"

Arthur remained silent for quite a while, trying Louise's patience. Ronald's words tumbled through Arthur's mind: "This depression sure 'as a way o' makin' monsters outa men....Desperate times call fer desperate measures."

Just as Louise was about to explode into a whirlwind of persuasive arguments, she heard a hoarsely whispered reply.

"Alright."

Chapter Twenty-Five:
Kidnapped

"Please, Pastor Olson?" begged Ruth late that evening. "Anna an' I wanna see 'im, too. We ain't seen 'im for a long time."

"Yes, of course. We'll pull you out of school for the day," Pastor Olson promised.

"Yay!" cheered Ruth as she danced around, her black curls springing with her. "We can see Uncle Arthur on Friday!"

"If he comes," Anna cautioned. "Thank you, Pastor Olson," she added, remembering her manners.

"Thank you!" cried Ruth, wrapping her arms around his neck. "I can't wait ta see Uncle Arthur!"

"I hope he's okay," fretted Rhoda. "Maybe we shouldn't have told him about Charity."

"You did nothing wrong," Pastor Olson stated firmly. "I'll tell you what. Let's pray for your uncle right now."

"What if he don't come?" asked Ruth in a quivering voice.

"We'll just have to wait and see," said Mrs. Olson, who was rocking steadily in her rocking chair, holding Elijah, who had fallen asleep more than an hour before.

◆　◆　◆

The Friday routine as volunteers at the soup kitchen was very much as it had been on Wednesday. Elijah escorted people—a job he liked very much—while Mrs. Olson cooked. Anna and Ruth helped serve the food, and Rhoda sat in her chair at the top of the stairs, knitting. Her fingers weren't nearly as quick when she was nervous. She tried her best to push the worry out of her mind, but it didn't seem to budge. *I hope Uncle Arthur will come today. I hope he's okay.*

Then she heard the woman.

"Come this way," Louise persuaded. "The surprise is just outside 'round the corner."

Rhoda heard the sound of feet climbing the stairs toward her. Her throat went dry as the woman and two others brushed past her.

"What's the surprise?" asked Dick.

"Can't tell you that," Louise said. "Come and see fer yourselves."

Rhoda heard the door open. Where was the woman taking the Maxwell boys? What could the surprise be? Something didn't seem right.

The door closed behind them. There was no time to get Mrs. Olson. Rhoda stumbled to her feet and felt for the doorknob.

"Help me, Jesus," she prayed quietly as she flung the door open.

Fixing her mind on what she was about to do, Rhoda kicked off her shoes and socks and felt the sidewalk with her bare toes. She concentrated on what the woman was saying up ahead.

"The surprise is right over here in the alleyway."

Rhoda flattened herself against the building and followed the voices toward the alley.

All of a sudden, the sound of scuffling reached Rhoda's ears.

"Lemme go!" demanded Andrew, his voice muffled.

Rhoda's heart nearly stopped, and her whole body became cold and clammy.

"You're comin' with us, you little chumps. Stop kicking!" Louise sneered.

Rhoda heard a man's voice, too, groaning in the struggle. Panic seized her. She had to do something! With her bare feet feeling the concrete, she thrust her arms out in front of her and started blindly running—yes, running—toward the alleyway, screaming for help at the top of her lungs. *Keep me on the path, Jesus*, she prayed.

Garbage cans clattered in the alley as someone jumped out and grabbed the woman. Rhoda heard her cursing and struggling to get free.

"It wasn't me, officers. It was him!" the woman shrieked. "He wanted ransom money. I tried to rescue these poor boys!"

"Aw, dry up," the officer replied dully as he handcuffed Louise.

Just then, a pair of arms grabbed Rhoda.

Chapter Twenty-Six:
Rhoda's Reward

Rhoda squirmed, twisted, and screamed in the man's vice-like grasp.

"Rhoda, stop struggling."

Uncle Arthur? Rhoda was dumbfounded. What was going on? Could Uncle Arthur be in on this? Her mind was whirling.

"Good work, Mr. Turner," a second officer commented as he untied the Maxwell boys. "If you hadn't come to tell us about Miss Harris' plan, she might have gotten away with it."

"You double-crosser!" Louise sputtered angrily. She continued to hurl insults as the officers led her away.

Arthur removed his arms from around Rhoda and took her hands in his. "Attagirl, Rhoda. Attagirl!"

"Uncle Arthur, I thought you were in on the kidnapping," Rhoda admitted. "I should've known better. I'm sor—"

"Louise told me her plan on Wednesday, and I secretly went to the police. They were planted here the whole time. I was told to play along with Miss Harris so they could catch her in the act."

A crowd of people poured out of the bank building to see what the commotion was all about.

"Rhoda," exclaimed Mrs. Olson rushing to her side, "are you hurt?"

"Why, Dick, Andrew, what are you doing out here?" demanded Lucille. "Oh, my!" she cried as the realization hit her. Lucille grew white and stumbled against a hobo who was able to catch her before she fell.

The whole story was relayed by Arthur to the crowd. He finished with, "It's a good thing Rhoda, here, has good ears

102

and a sharp mind. She understood the danger and ran out here like a wildcat."

"Ith my thithter a hero?"

"Yes, she is. She's very brave."

"I wasn't brave. I was plenty scared not knowin' where I was going, but I asked Jesus to help me, an' He did."

♦   ♦   ♦

"Mrs. Olson, if I wasn't blind, maybe I wouldn't have been in the right place at the right time. Maybe I wouldn't have heard what was going on. Maybe this ain't the whole reason that God made me blind, but God sure used it for good today."

Rebecca agreed and dished more casserole onto Arthur's plate. He had been invited to supper. The conversation turned to Charity, and the children spent a good deal of time telling Arthur the news since his departure from home.

"I just don't have the clams for a doctor," Arthur sighed. "I can't even afford a train ticket home."

"The Lord is still able when we are not," said Pastor Olson, just as the doorbell rang. "Excuse me." He rose from the table to open the door. "Please, come in."

Lucille wasted no time hurrying over to Rhoda's place at the dinner table. "I came face-to-face with losing my boys before I realized how much they mean to me." Lucille paused before continuing. "We—Walter and I—want to give you a reward. We insist. How can we repay you?"

Rhoda was astounded. *A reward? For me?* "I think God is answering our prayers right now, Uncle Arthur. I know just what I want! I want a train ticket for my uncle."

"Rhoda, this isn't a reward for me. It's for you."

"Wait, you're her uncle? Aren't you Mr. Turner?" asked Lucille, recognizing him. "Aren't you the one who helped the police rescue my boys? Now, what's all this about a train ticket?"

James explained the Turners' situation to the Maxwells.

"Mr. Turner, consider that train ticket yours," Walter stated. "And submit that doctor bill to me, too."

Arthur tried to respond. Instead, he clasped Walter Maxwell's hand in both of his and pumped it up and down briskly.

"Now, Rhoda, is there nothing we can give you?" Mrs. Maxwell inquired.

"No, ma'am. I just want Charity to be better an' Uncle Arthur to be back home. That makes me happy."

"But surely there's something you might like. Some new dresses perhaps?"

Rhoda cringed at the very thought of another store-bought dress. "No, thank you. The only other thing I wish for is…well…is," Rhoda hesitated, and then her deepest yearning came forth in a rush. "I sure wish I could go to school. I wanna learn so much. I wanna be able to read again. I wanna read the Bible for myself whenever I want to." With a sigh, Rhoda concluded, "But I can't, an' you ain't able to give me back my sight no matter how much money you have."

"No…no, we can't," Lucille agreed with sincere sympathy in her voice for perhaps the first time in her life. Suddenly, she clapped her hands to her chin as an idea wriggled its way into her mind. She pulled Walter aside for an impromptu whispered conference.

Upon their return, Lucille announced, "What would you think about going to a school for the blind? There's a state boarding school eighty miles from here. Tuition is free, and we would be delighted to pay for any incidentals as well as for transportation back and forth for visits home. Perhaps a certain bank could make a donation to the school, and maybe a certain bank owner could bring up your name in conversation to ensure your admission and make things quite comfortable for you."

"Why, that's bribery!" blurted Arthur.

"Well, money talks."

Rhoda's jaw dropped as she tried to comprehend what she was hearing. "School? A school for the blind? Oh, I hope

Mother will let me. I can't believe it. I might be able to go to school!"

Chapter Twenty-Seven:
Reunited

"Please, Mama?" begged Charity. "It's so nice out, an' I ain't been outside forever."

"No, Charity. I want you to rest for a few days before you go traipsing around outside."

"Can't I rest outside?" Charity pleaded. "I won't climb any trees or go runnin' around or nothin'."

"Well, alright. The fresh air might do you some good," relented Bette. "But remember, you're only resting. No playing today."

"Thank you!" Charity flung open the back door. She felt like a bird released from its cage.

Charity meandered around the yard, smelled flowers, felt tree bark, and basked in the sunshine. As she sat on the ground picking at the grass to amuse herself, an approaching figure caught her eye. She squinted to try to recognize the face.

"Charity!" the man's voice rang out.

"Daddy!" Knowing that nobody would mind if she disobeyed Mama's restrictions on such an occasion, she leaped up and ran full-tilt into his arms.

"Charity, I've been so worried about you!"

"Daddy, are you really home? Am I dreaming? So much has happened since you left." Charity became very serious. "Daddy, Rhoda's blind. She was really sick—"

"I know."

"You do?"

"I heard you were very sick, too, but look at you! Oh, thank God."

The door opened, and Bette tore out of the house to embrace her husband.

"My sweet Bette." Arthur kissed his wife. "Boy, have I got a story to tell you!"

Chapter Twenty-Eight:
A Visitor

Saturday morning was fresh and bright. The day had no difficulty drawing the Olsons and the Clayton children outdoors. The baking, laundry, cleaning, and sermon outline could wait.

Mrs. Olson took the opportunity to weed a section in her flower garden, while Elijah dug for worms and Pastor Olson trimmed bushes with his pruners.

Anna and Ruth busied themselves trying to teach Rhoda how to jump rope. Multiple tries and falls later, Rhoda finally managed to jump throughout an entire rhyme. Everyone clapped and Rhoda was radiant.

"I liked to jump rope when I was a girl," Mrs. Olson mentioned casually.

"Show us," urged Ruth excitedly.

"I'd like to see this," commented Pastor Olson slyly, as he put down the pruners.

"Don't be ridiculous. That was a long time ago."

"It wasn't that long ago," coaxed Pastor Olson. "Why don't you give it a try?"

Reluctantly, Mrs. Olson agreed. She took off her gardening gloves and shoes.

"Ladies and gentlemen, Rebecca Olson, jump rope queen," Pastor Olson joked.

Mrs. Olson was successful, and Pastor Olson was obviously quite pleased.

"Let's see Rhoda do it again," Mrs. Olson puffed. "I'm beat!"

Everyone was so busy watching Rhoda jump that none of them except Rhoda heard the approaching footsteps.

"Is someone coming?" she asked.

"Mother!" Ruth shouted. In a whirl of excitement, jump ropes flew in a tangle, worms were trampled underfoot, and all of the Clayton children crowded around the woman who gathered them in her arms.

"I've missed you so much! And Rhoda. Is this my Rhoda?"

"It's me, Mother," she assured her anxiously. "Can't you recognize me?"

"Hardly!" Mother replied, studying her. "You're not nearly as pale and...and you were jumping rope!" Mother's words came out slowly, as though she were trying to process the truth of them. "How can it be?"

"Jesus helps me," Rhoda replied matter-of-factly. "He takes care of me, an' I ain't afraid. He has a plan for me, Mother. I can't wait to tell you everything!"

"James, Rebecca, you have no idea how wonderful...I mean...I can't thank...I..."

"The Lord works in mysterious ways," Rebecca replied simply. "And you'll never know what a blessing your children have been to us," she finished with a catch in her own voice.

"Ith Charity better?" Elijah butted in.

"Her fever broke on Thursday night, and she's doing much better. Both she and Aunt Bette want me to say 'hello' to all of you."

"Yay!" Ruth cheered. "We were all praying that she would get better soon."

"Uncle Arthur will be tho happy when he getth home."

"Yes, I'm sure he will be some day."

"No, Mother, he's on his way there now!" Anna explained.

"What? Have I missed something? Am I on another planet?"

"Let's all go inside," Pastor Olson suggested. "Looks like we have lots to talk about!"

For the rest of the day, Mother shared news about Charity and Aunt Bette, while the children filled Mother in on their adventures.

Repeatedly, Pauline expressed to the Olsons, "How can I ever thank you?"

A blanket-bed for Anna was made up on the attic floor so Mother could have Anna's cot that night. Elijah was strangely quiet as he followed Pastor Olson around wherever he went. Pastor Olson played with Elijah all evening, knowing he would miss the little boy as much as Elijah would miss him.

Pauline and Rebecca helped the children pack their belongings. Mother was amazed when she saw the small pile of scarves and hats that Rhoda had knitted for the soup kitchen.

"Be sure to take them, Mrs. Olson."

"Don't worry, Rhoda. I'll take them to the soup kitchen on Monday," she promised.

"Will you and Pastor Olson visit us at our house sometime?" begged Ruth.

"We wouldn't have it any other way."

"Hog diggity dog!" Elijah proclaimed from the floor where he and Pastor Olson were playing with Elijah's wooden train.

"And we can write letters to the Olsons, too, can't we?" Anna added.

"Yes, Anna. We'll be sure to keep in touch." Mother stuffed a shirt into Elijah's bulging carpetbag. "I declare, Rebecca, it'll be a miracle if I can get them onto the train tomorrow."

♦　　♦　　♦

On Sunday morning, the crew went to church together before the Olsons drove the Claytons to the train station. This time, much to the pleasure of them both, Elijah was allowed to sit by Pastor Olson during the service—right at his feet by the pulpit. And, for the very first time, Rhoda listened wholeheartedly to the entire sermon.

"Before we close," Pastor Olson said, "Let's sing the first verse of 'Amazing Grace.'"

Rhoda had never heard the song before. She carefully listened to the words as voices rang out in harmony.

> Amazing grace, how sweet the sound,
> That saved a wretch like me.
> I once was lost but now am found,
> Was blind, but now I see.

"Was blind, but now I see," Rhoda repeated softly to herself. She fingered the shell necklace that hung around her neck. The words she had spoken to Charity came back to her. *No, Charity, nothing will ever be the same!* Rhoda smiled.

The problem:

Romans 3:23: For all have sinned, and come short of the glory of God.

Romans 6:23a: For the wages of sin is death... [Death means separation from God forever. See also Revelation 20:13-15.]

You can't fix the problem yourself.

Romans 3:20: Therefore by the deeds of the law [being good / doing good] there shall no flesh be justified in his sight: for by the law is the knowledge of sin. [The more we understand about God's standard of perfect holiness, the more we realize how far short we fall. We are condemned. See also Romans 3:10.]

Ephesians 2:9: [The way to heaven is not through your own good deeds; it is:] not of works, lest any man should boast. [See also Isaiah 64:6 and Titus 3:5-7.]

God has solved the problem *for* you.

Romans 5:8: But God commendeth his love toward us, in that, while we were yet sinners, Christ died for us. [God loves you so much that He willingly came to earth to take a punishment He didn't deserve in order to settle the debt you are unable to pay. See also Colossians 2:13-14.]

Isaiah 53:5: But he [Jesus Christ] was wounded for our transgressions, he was bruised for our iniquities: the chastisement of our peace was upon him; and with his stripes we are healed.

1 Corinthians 15:3b-4: ...Christ died for our sins according to the scriptures; and that he was buried and that he rose again the third day according to the scriptures...

What must you do to be rescued?

John 3:16: For God so loved the world, that he gave his only begotten Son [Jesus], that whosoever believeth in him should not perish, but have everlasting life. [If you trust that Christ's sacrifice on your behalf is sufficient to pay off your sin-debt, you are no longer condemned, but saved! See also Romans 6:23b and Romans 8:1-3.]

To the only wise God our Saviour, be glory and majesty, dominion and power, both now and ever. Amen. [Jude 1:25]